BIGGLES BREAKS THE SILENCE

Ginger stared down as the machine skimmed low in a trial run. The surface looked perfect – hard, and as flat as a bowling green. He could see no obstruction. There was no wind, so the question of direction did not arise.

Biggles turned the aircraft and allowed it gently to lose height. He flattened out. Ginger held his breath. Nothing happened. Then his nerves twitched as the engines roared again and the machine swung up in a climbing turn.

Biggles laughed, a short laugh without any humour in it. 'See what I mean,' he muttered. 'I thought I was on the carpet, but I must have flattened out about ten feet too high. Landing on snow is always tricky, but here, in this grey light, where there's nothing else but snow, it's definitely nasty.'

About the author

Captain W. E. Johns, who died in 1968 at the age of 75, served with considerable distinction in the R.F.C. in World War 1. After working with the R.A.F. in peacetime he became a prominent Air Correspondent and author of aviation books, and in 1932 he founded the magazine *Popular Flying*. Biggles first appeared in short stories in the same year, a character who was typical of the kind of man Captain Johns knew in the War.

Altogether Captain Johns wrote 85 books about Biggles, who has now become one of the most famous characters in children's fiction.

Biggles Breaks the Silence

Captain W. E. Johns

KNIGHT BOOKS
Hodder and Stoughton

First published in 1949 by Hodder & Stoughton Ltd.

Knight Books edition 1983

British Library C.I.P.
Johns, W.E.
Biggles breaks the silence.—(Knight books)
I. Title
823'.912[J]　　PZ7

ISBN 0-340-33687-0

The characters and situations in this book are entirely imaginary and bear no relation to any real person or actual happening.

Printed and bound in Great Britain for Hodder and Stoughton Paperbacks, a division of Hodder and Stoughton Ltd., Mill Road, Dunton Green, Sevenoaks, Kent (Editorial Office: 47 Bedford Square, London, WC1 3DP) by Cox and Wyman Ltd., Cardiff Road, Reading.

The story of the *Starry Crown* is one of the unsolved mysteries of the sea. This adventure is based on facts, so far as they are known, though the re-discovery of the wreck and treasure, and the characters of Biggles, his friends and enemies, are purely fictitious.

CONTENTS

CHAPTER I

BIGGLES HAS VISITORS

'As a job, ours is about the dullest ever. What's the use of having Air Police if there are no air crooks?' Air Constable 'Ginger' Hebblethwaite, of the Air Section, Criminal Investigation Department, New Scotland Yard, considered with moody impatience two of his colleagues, who were regarding him with sympathetic toleration from the depths of the arm-chairs in which they had slumped. One was Algy Lacey, and the other Lord Bertie Lissie, who for the purpose of his present duties had dropped his title.

Bertie polished his monocle with a screw of paper torn from the journal he had been reading. 'Absolutely, old boy. I couldn't agree with you more,' he agreed sadly.

'In the matter of entertainment it looks as if we shall soon be reduced to feeding the pigeons in Trafalgar Square,' observed Algy, yawning.

'For a bunch of disgruntled spivs you'd be hard to beat. Some people would call you lucky, being paid for doing nothing.' The voice came from the other side of the room, where Sergeant Biggleśworth, head of the Department, was regarding the street below through the window of his London flat in Mount Street, Mayfair. 'After all,' he went on, 'there were some air crooks when we started, which is why the air section was formed.'

'I know; but our mistake was we were in too much of

a hurry to liquidate them,' grumbled Ginger.

'We did what we were paid to do,' Biggles pointed out.

'We left ourselves with nothing to do.'

'What's wrong with that? Can't you rest?'

'I shall have plenty of time to rest when I am drawing the Old Age Pension,' muttered Ginger.

'At the rate you're fretting yourself to death you'll be lucky to see the colour of that money,' asserted Biggles cynically. 'But just a minute. Don't get excited, but I fancy we're going to have visitors.'

'What gave you that idea?'

'I can see two people coming along the pavement.'

'What makes you think they're coming here?'

'Deduction, my dear sir, deduction. As detectives our job is to deduct.'

'Then what about deducting a few pounds from the bank and going somewhere,' suggested Ginger.

'We may have to do that presently,' replied Biggles. 'I told you I could see two men on their way here. At any rate, they're looking at the numbers of the doors, and I've seen one of them before.'

'Where?'

'I don't know. I've seen too many faces in my time to remember them all.'

'What does this chap look like?'

'Young, clean-shaven, smart, fair-haired, walks as though he had been in one of the services.'

'That description would fit just about a million fellows in London to-day,' observed Ginger with mild sarcasm.

Biggles ignored the remark. 'The man with him is much older. Looks like a naval type. Yes, they're at the door.'

Biggles turned away from the window smiling faintly. 'You can now amuse yourselves trying to guess where this visit will ultimately land us,' he added. 'You'll have noticed that our callers usually want us to go somewhere and do something.'

'The penalty of fame, old boy, the penalty of fame,' murmured Bertie softly.

'Well, I'm game for anywhere bar the North Pole,' declared Ginger.

'Absolutely,' asserted Bertie. 'Beastly place. Frightfully cold, and all that. No hot water for a bath. Miles and miles of absolutely nothing at all — so I've been told.'

There came a tap on the door, which was opened to admit the face of Biggles' housekeeper. 'Two gentlemen to see you, sir,' she announced.

'Thank you, Mrs Symes. Bring them in,' requested Biggles.

The visitors entered slowly, and, it seemed, a trifle nervously. The first was the fresh-complexioned lad whom Biggles had roughly described. The other was much older, a shortish, heavily-built man, with a rugged, square-cut face in which were set two of the bluest eyes Ginger had ever seen. He wore a dark blue reefer jacket with brass buttons, and carried in his hands a faded peaked cap.

Biggles indicated convenient chairs. 'Please sit down,' he invited. 'My name is Bigglesworth. I gather you want to speak to me.'

The younger of the two answered, in a Clydeside accent. 'Yes, sir. You remember me, sir — L.A.C. Grimes, fitter aero. I was in your Squadron in the Western Desert. The boys used to call me Grimy.'

Biggles' eyes opened wide. 'Of course. I knew I had

seen you before, but I couldn't remember where. One meets a lot of people in the Service.' He held out a hand. 'How's civil life treating you?'

'Oh, not bad, sir,' was the ready answer. 'I've got a little business of my own, a bicycle shop, in Glasgow. Trouble is, I can't get the bikes. I've brought my father along to see you. He wants — well, we both want— a bit of advice. I couldn't think of anyone better than you to ask. Hope you don't mind, sir.'

'Not in the least,' returned Biggles quickly. 'What can I do for you?'

The ex-airman looked at his father. 'You tell him, guv'nor,' he urged.

Biggles turned to the older man. 'Been in the Navy?'

Grimes, senior, cleared his throat. 'Merchant Navy, sir,' he answered, in the rich Glasgow accent. 'Jumbo Grimes they call me, in the ports where sailors meet.'

'Why Jumbo?' inquired Biggles curiously.

The old man looked a trifle embarrassed. 'I once had to bring an elephant home from Bombay for the London Zoo. He didn't want to come. When we were at sea he got loose and sort of stirred things up a bit. The story got out and I've been Jumbo ever since.'

Biggles nodded, smiling. 'I see. And what's the trouble now?'

The sailor looked doubtful. 'It's a long story.'

'No matter. We're in no hurry. Take your time.'

'Well, sir, it's like this,' explained the sailor. 'I reckon I know where there's a pile of money waiting to be picked up.'

Biggles nodded slowly. 'I see. So in your travels you've tumbled on a treasure trove, eh, and you'd like to get it under your hatches.'

'Aye, that's right.'

'And what am I supposed to do about it?'

The old sailor looked a little taken aback at the directness of Biggles' question. 'Well — er — I thought, mebbe —'

His son helped him out. 'We thought you might give us advice. I didn't know who else to ask.'

'What you really mean is, you thought I might do something about it myself,' suggested Biggles shrewdly. 'Am I right?'

L.A.C. Grimes moistened his lips nervously. 'Yes, sir. I reckon that's about the size of it.'

'You know, I suppose, that treasure hunts usually fail.'

'Well, it would be fun anyway,' averred Grimy.

'Very expensive fun for the man who provides the transport and foots the bills,' Biggles pointed out. 'But let's forget that for a moment,' he went on, selecting a cigarette from his case and tapping it on the back of his hand. 'Where exactly is this pile of wealth?'

Grimes, senior, answered. 'It's down near the South Pole,' he said weakly.

Biggles stared. 'Holy Smoke! That sounds like a tall order. Are you sure you're not making a mistake? I mean, what lunatic would bury a pile of gold in the South Pole?'

'Well, it isn't exactly a pile of gold,' admitted the sailor, looking somewhat crestfallen.

'What is it, then?'

'It's a crown.'

'A *what*?'

'A crown. A gold crown with diamonds in it.'

Biggles frowned. 'That doesn't make sense to me,' he asserted. 'How, may I ask, did a diamond-studded crown get to the South Pole? Have you seen it?'

'No.'

'Are you sure it's there?'

'Well, I'm not sure about the diamonds, but—'

The son, apparently not at all happy about the way things were going, chipped in. 'Tell him about it, guv'nor,' he urged.

Biggles dropped into a chair. 'Go ahead, we're listening,' he said, offering his cigarette case.

'Not for me, thanks, but I'll take a draw at my pipe, if it is all the same to you,' answered the sailor. He took from his pocket an old-fashioned silver-banded pipe, and from a coil of black plug tobacco cut with a ferocious-looking jack-knife a few slices, which he thumbed well in before applying the flame produced by a massive brass petrol lighter. He then emitted a blue reek of smoke of such pungency that Ginger backed hastily, stifling a cough.

'Well sir, this was the way of it,' began the seaman. 'I was homeward bound from Shanghai when the Japs came into the war. My ship was seized and I was sent to a prison camp for the duration. The less said about that the better. When the war was over I had to see about getting home, but there was a lot of people besides me and not enough transport, which meant a waiting list. While I was waiting my turn in Hong Kong a fellow came to see me. His name was Lavinsky—or so he said, and it may be true for all I know. His nationality was a matter of guesswork. I could tell that from the way he talked. He spoke English well enough, although he certainly wasn't British. He mentioned one day that he was an Australian, but he didn't look like one to me. He was a bit too friendly with the Japs for my liking, too, but he explained that by saying he was in business in the Far East before the war, and I suppose that could have been true. Anyhow, he had a proposition to make, and this was it. He had got a ship, which he had sold to the Chilean Government provided he could deliver it to Santiago. I believed it at the time because I had no reason not to, and it sounded reasonable enough, but in view of what happened later I reckon that was all just a pack of lies. He was no sailor himself, you understand. He was looking for someone who held a master's ticket, and was willing to pay him well for taking the ship over. He'd be coming along as a passenger, he said. Well, it sounded fair enough, and as I had nothing better to do I said I'd go and cast an eye over this craft. One look should have told me that the whole thing was fishy, for of all the antiquated tubs I've ever seen she was about the worst. Her name was the *Svelt*, a Danish schooner with Italian engines, one of which wouldn't work and the other looked as though it would drop through the bottom any minute. My first impression was to have nothing to do with her, and I would have been right; but Lavinsky told me he had a Scots engineer, which was true enough, and he would see that everything was all right before we started. Apart from that, I thought it might be easier to get home from South America than from China.' The sailor relighted his pipe, which had gone out.

'Well, three weeks later we put to sea with as motley a crew as ever stepped on board ship — men of every race and colour. Lavinsky had certainly collected the scum of the water-fronts. Not that that worried me. I learnt my trade in the old school and I'd handled tough crews before. The only other man I'd trust was Neil McArthur, my chief engineer, God rest him. He also was fed up with hanging about Hong Kong. Lavinsky was there, with, if you please, a couple of Jap passengers who wanted — so he said — to get to South America. I didn't know they were below until we were well out of the harbour or I'd have put them ashore. Two smug guys they were — fairly fawned on me from the start. Not that that took me in for a minute. Not likely. It wasn't long before I twigged that these two beauties were the real owners of the ship. Lavinsky was only a stooge. I couldn't pronounce their real names, so I called them Shim and Sham for short. That was as near as I could get.

'Well, for a time it was all plain sailing. We had fair weather and it looked as if everything was going to be all right after all. Then Lavinsky started to take a particular interest in the ship's position. Trouble started when we were getting pretty close to our destination. Lavinsky came to me on the bridge and told me to take up a new course south. I asked him what for. He said there'd been a change of plan and his owners wanted him to run to Graham Land. When I'd recovered from the shock, I asked him what in thunder he expected to find in Graham Land, which sticks out from the Atlantic ice pack. He said that was a private matter, but I should know all about it in due course. I said it wasn't in the contract, but he said he would make it right with me as far as money went. I didn't like it, and I said so. I began to smell a rat and an ugly one at that. I went below and had a word with Neil — Lavinsky and the rest of the crew watching me all the time. It began to look as if me and Neil were the only people on the ship who didn't know the real object of the voyage. Well, we could see there was going to be trouble if we refused to accept orders from the owners. I was thinking about my ticket. There wasn't a man on board who could have brought the ship to port without me and Neil, and had the ship been piled up somewhere there would have been a row over the insurance which might have put me ashore for good. Well, to make a long story short, I agreed to the new orders, but I made a note in the log that I did it under protest. The result was, a fortnight later we were groping our way through the big bergs and drift ice of the Bellingshausen Sea. When the real polar ice brought us to a stop I said, well, here we are, and I hope you like the scenery. What do we do next. But I'll tell you one thing, I said; if we get caught here in this ice your ship will crack apart like a matchbox under a steam-roller, and you'll have no more chance of getting home than a fly in a treacle jar.' The sailor thumbed the bowl of his pipe vigorously.

'Well, it didn't take me long to see what the game was,' he resumed. 'Seals. I had hitched up with a gang of seal poachers. I told Lavinsky what I thought about him and his pals. We had a first-class row, but with the whole ship's company against us, what could me and Neil do about it except threaten to report them when we got home. Mebbe I wasn't wise in saying that, as I realised later. We had still got to get home. Lavinsky offered me a share of the profits if I'd keep my mouth shut, but I told him I wouldn't touch his dirty money with the end of the mainmast. Things looked ugly. Meanwhile, the slaughter of seals went on, and this was the state of affairs when a queer thing happened, something that put a new complexion on the whole expedition. We were drifting along near the ice ready to get out the moment we looked like getting caught, when, lo and behold, what do we see but the masts of a schooner sticking up out of the ice some distance back from the open water. She was fast in the pack, no doubt of that. Lavinsky went off to find out what ship it was.

Shim and Sham went with him.

'They were away about a couple of hours, and when they came back I could see that something had happened. They were as white as ghosts and had a funny sort of wild look in their eyes. I asked them what they'd found, and they said nothing but an old hulk. There was nothing worth salvaging. I, of course, asked them for the name of the ship so that I could enter it in the log. Lavinsky said he couldn't make out the name, she was so smothered up in ice and snow — which was another lie, if ever I heard one. After that he couldn't get away from the place fast enough, which suited me, though I'd have given something to know what they'd found.'

Biggles interrupted the narrative. 'I take it they brought nothing back with them?'

'Not a thing. I'm sure of that.'

'But if they'd found something worth having they would hardly be likely to leave it behind,' Biggles pointed out.

'I think that's where you're wrong,' said the sailor thoughtfully. 'Had it been some jimcrack stuff they'd have brought it along, no doubt. But this was something big, and they didn't trust me. It wouldn't do for me to know what they'd found — not on your life. Anyway, there it was. I had orders to go back to Hong Kong. I didn't argue. I'd have gone anywhere to get off that crooked ship.

'A few nights later Neil came to me in my cabin. There was a funny look on his face. He said to me; "Do you know what Lavinsky found in that wreck?" I said "No." He said, "Well, I do. They found a gold crown studded with diamonds." I said, "How do you know that?" He said, "I've been listening to them talking outside Lavinsky's cabin. They were talking Japanese, but I happen to know a bit of the lingo, and made out something about a crown of diamonds." '

At this point Biggles again interrupted. 'But that doesn't make sense,' he protested. 'No one would take a diamond-studded crown to the Antarctic; and, anyway, if one had been lost the world would have been told about it. Was Neil quite sure about these words — crown and diamonds?'

The sailor hesitated. 'Well, not exactly. The words were stars and crown, but he reckoned that stars could only mean diamonds.'

Suddenly a strange expression came into Biggles' eyes. 'Just a minute,' he said slowly. 'Just a minute. Stars and crown, eh? That rings a bell in my memory. Never mind. Go ahead. We'll come back to this presently.'

Jumbo Grimes, the sailor of the seven seas, continued. 'As we drew nearer to our home port I could sense a nasty sort of feeling on the ship. Mebbe it was the way Lavinsky and his pals kept clear of me, or the way the crew took to muttering in little groups. I sent for Neil. "Neil, we know too much," I said. "This crew isn't going to let us ashore knowing what we know. They'll go to jail for seal-poaching, and they know it as well as we do. Keep your eyes skinned for trouble. It'll come, I reckon when we are close enough to port for these rats to handle the ship for themselves." I was right, too, dead right. The night before we were due to dock Neil rang me on the telegraph to say that he was coming on deck for a breather and to have a word. Things were looking pretty nasty, he said. He never came. A few minutes later I heard a splash. I didn't pay much attention to it then, but as time went on and Neil didn't come I had an uneasy feeling what had happened. When I went below to find Neil he wasn't there. He wasn't in his cabin, either. Then I knew they'd heaved him overboard. So that's it, I thought. No doubt I'm next on the list. Well, I said to myself, we'll see about that. I slipped into my cabin and got the gun I always carry. When I got back to the deck there they were, waiting for me. What was I to do? Well, it didn't take me long to make up my mind. I couldn't hope to fight the whole bunch and get away with it. I knew that. So I blazed a couple of shots at them and then went overboard. We weren't far from land and I'm a pretty strong swimmer. It was pitch dark, and although they put a boat down to look for me I gave them the slip. I swam to the shore. It took me some time to make my way up the coast to Hong Kong, and when I got there I found that the *Svelt* had been in and gone. Lavinsky, I learned, had been looking for me. I told what I knew to the British Agent. What did it amount to? Mighty little. Anyway, the authorities had plenty to do, clearing up after the Jap occupation, without worrying their heads about a wild yarn such as mine must have sounded.' The sailor pocketed his pipe.

'Well, sir, that's about all,' he concluded. 'I was offered a chance to get home on the next boat and I took it. I told my boy here what I have told you, and he seemed to think that if we could get out to this old hulk we might pick up — well, some valuable salvage. The question was how to get there. Grimy said you might give us your opinion. You might even know someone who would — sort of — help us.'

A ghost of a smile crossed Biggles' face. 'I see,' he said softly.

'There is one thing I am sure of,' declared the sailor.

'Lavinsky didn't bring the crown away with him.'

'I'm quite sure of that, too,' said Biggles drily.

The mariner looked puzzled. 'Why are *you* so sure of that?'

'Because,' answered Biggles slowly, 'the crown he found would be too big, much too big, for him to handle.'

CHAPTER 2

A PAGE FROM THE PAST

Captain Grimes stared at Biggles as if he doubted his sanity. 'I don't know what you're talking about,' he stated, with some asperity. 'How could a gold crown—'

'I'm not talking about a gold crown,' interposed Biggles quickly. 'There isn't a gold crown in the Antarctic, and there never was. Your assumption that there is one, or was one, is natural enough; but it was, after all, only surmise on your part. I suspect that the crown that Lavinsky found was a wooden one.' Biggles paused to smile at the expression on the seaman's face. 'You see, skipper,' he continued, 'unless I've missed my guess, what Lavinsky blundered on was the remains of an old schooner named the *Starry Crown*.'

Captain Grimes drew a deep breath. He looked crestfallen. 'Never heard of her,' he muttered.

'Very few people have, I imagine,' returned Biggles. 'I happen to have done so because unsolved mysteries have always interested me, and I pay a press-cutting agency to keep me informed about them or any subsequent developments. The *Starry Crown* sailed the seas in another generation. If my memory isn't at fault, she disappeared from sight many years ago, on a voyage from Australia to London.'

'Well, knock me down with a marlinespike,' exclaimed the old man disconsolately. 'Here am I kidding myself I'm on the track of a fortune.'

Biggles smiled again at the sailor's frank expression

of chagrin. 'I didn't say you weren't,' he corrected. 'In fact, you probably are.'

The sailor looked up sharply, his shrewd eyes narrowing. 'Ah! Then there is something.'

'There was, and in view of what you now tell us, I'd say there still is. When the *Starry Crown* set sail she had on board about a ton of Australian gold, although how much of it remains under her hatches is another matter. Just a moment while I turn up my scrap-book; we might as well get our facts right.' Biggles went over to his files and put on the table a bulky album, from which the edges of newspaper clippings projected at all angles. He turned the pages slowly, and then apparently found what he was looking for, for he opened the book wide and read for some minutes in silence. 'Yes,' he said at last. 'I wasn't far wrong. The *Starry Crown* was a queer business altogether. She was a schooner of fifteen hundred tons. With a ton of gold on board she disappeared on a voyage from Melbourne to London. She was reported lost with all hands, and eventually the insurance money was paid. But that wasn't the end of the story. Twenty years later a whaler named *Swordfish* spotted the *Starry Crown* stuck fast in the polar ice-pack. The *Swordfish* herself was in a bad way. She had been driven south by northerly gales and her crew was down with scurvy. In fact, there was only one survivor, the mate, a man named Last. He died in Australia some years ago. It seems that after he got home he took into his confidence a man named Manton, presumably because he was the owner of a schooner, a vessel named *Black Dog*. The upshot was, naturally enough, that Last and Manton went off in the *Black Dog* to recover the *Starry Crown*'s gold. Things went wrong, as they usually do in treasure hunting. The *Black Dog* was caught between two bergs and crushed flat. The only two men to get ashore were Last and Manton. They may have been on the ice at the time. At any rate, after the *Black Dog* had gone down they were able to walk across the ice to the *Starry Crown*. They found things just the same as when the ship had been abandoned. The gold was intact, not that it was much use to the wretched fellows, who now found themselves prisoners on the Antarctic ice with mighty little hope of ever getting away. There was still a good supply of canned stores in the hulk, and other food which had been preserved by the intense cold, so they were in no immediate danger of starvation; but winter was setting in and their chances of being picked up were nil. To pass the time they amused themselves by dividing the gold between them. After some months the solitude drove Manton out of his mind, and he tried to murder Last. There was a fight, and it ended by Last shooting Manton dead. He buried him in the ice, built a cairn of ice blocks over his grave, and topped it with a board with the dead man's name on it. This done, to save himself being driven insane by the loneliness, he repaired the one small boat that remained on the *Starry Crown*. He then built a sledge, loaded the boat with some stores, and in the spring, when the ice began to break up, dragged the whole thing to the edge of the open water. All this occupied eight months. But his luck was in, for shortly afterwards he was picked up by an American whaler named *Spray*. He told the skipper some cock-and-bull story about losing his ship and being cast away, and eventually got home. But he never fully recovered and he died shortly afterwards. Before he died, however, he told the story of his adventures to a relation, who might well have wondered how much of it was true. Later on, apparently, this man told some friends about it, and the story got out, which is how we know what I'm telling you now. Of course, how much truth there is in it we don't know. Most people would probably take Last's story with a ladleful of salt. He may have tried to cover up some unsavoury event in his career. He may have gone really mad, like Manton, and imagined things. Anyway, as far as I know, no attempt has ever been made to check up on his story, presumably because nobody thought it worth while; but now, skipper, in view of what you tell us, it begins to look as though there was something in it. If the *Starry Crown* is still there, then the gold is probably there, too.'

'Didn't Last take any of it away with him?' asked Ginger.

'Apparently not. Would you, in such circumstances, load yourself up with a lot of useless weight? The man had plenty to haul over the ice as it was. His one concern, I imagine, was to save his life, and his hopes of that must have looked pretty thin.' Biggles closed the book. 'Well, that's all — so far. I say so far, because it looks as if the final chapter has still to be told, assuming that the *Starry Crown* is still there.' He turned to Captain Grimes. 'Did you make a note of her position?'

'Of course.'

'Did you tell Lavinsky?'

'No.'

'But he could have got your own position from the log?'

'He may have done that later, but, even so, as we were drifting all the time the position he got when we were near the *Starry Crown* would only be approximate.'

'Was the ice moving? I ask that because, if it was, the *Starry Crown* would naturally move with it. I understand that in the spring enormous fields of ice on the edge of the main pack break off and shift about.'

'That's right enough,' agreed the captain. 'It's the big danger any ship has to face — getting caught between two floes. The weight would crush any ship as flat as a pancake. There's no doubt the outer ice was on the move when I was there, but such movements are naturally slow. What you've got to watch, when you're close in, is that a piece doesn't get between you and the open sea and shut you in. That's what must have happened to the *Starry Crown*. It very nearly caught me.'

Biggles lit another cigarette. 'Well, there it is,' he murmured. 'It looks as if the gold is still there — provided Lavinsky and Co. haven't slipped back and lifted it. What are you going to do about it?'

The sailor looked helpless. 'What can I do? I reckon Lavinsky will be after it all right.'

'No doubt of that. Most men are ready to take risks when the prize is gold.'

'The gold isn't his.'

'It isn't yours, if it comes to that,' Biggles pointed out. 'What puzzles me is, why didn't Lavinsky lift it when he was there?'

'There wasn't time, or mebbe they would have done,' stated the sailor. 'The ice was closing in on me and they only just got aboard in time, as it was; but, of course, they'll go back. And they won't waste any time, either, I'll bet my sea-boots.'

'And you had an idea that you might beat them to it — by flying down, eh,' murmured Biggles. 'Was that what brought you here?'

The sailor looked uncomfortable. 'You've about hit the nail on the head,' he admitted.

'But before you, or anyone, could do anything, it

would be necessary to determine the ownership of the gold,' averred Biggles.

'I reckon the stuff would belong to the underwriters who insured the ship, unless they sold the salvage,' opined Captain Grimes. 'The salvage wouldn't be much at the time, as the ship was reckoned to be at the bottom of the sea.'

'Quite so. But if the owners of the salvage knew that the ship was still afloat, so to speak, with the gold on board, it would be a very different matter. Have you told anyone else about this?'

'Not a soul. After all, I didn't know about the *Starry Crown* until you just told me. All I reported was the seal poaching.'

'Then the first thing to do is to ascertain the ownership of the salvage and find out if it is for sale. If it is, you must buy it. You ought to get it for a mere song. After that all you have to do is to go down and collect the bullion.'

The sailor looked doubtful. 'I couldn't do it — not alone. I could't afford such a trip. Anyway, to go by ship would take too long. I should probably find that Lavinsky had been there and gone. He'll be on his way there by now.'

Biggles nodded. 'I'm afraid you're right. Lavinsky would soon be on the job.'

'He'd have to find a better ship than the *Svelt*. She was dropping to bits and the engines were about done. But there, no doubt he'd soon find another ship.'

'I'm not so sure of that,' returned Biggles. 'Ships are expensive things. I doubt if such a man would have enough money to buy one.'

'He'd soon borrow one.'

'I don't think so.'

'Why not?'

'Because when Lavinsky went looking for a ship the owner would want to know what he wanted it for. Would Lavinsky tell him? I think it's unlikely, because as soon as he mentioned treasure the owner would want a finger in the pie. Remember, on these jaunts it's the man who puts up the money who calls the tune. Lavinsky would jib at taking second place, and from what you tell me of him, he isn't the sort of man to hand over half the profits. No; if he's gone after the gold, rather than divulge what he knows to a stranger he'd use his old ship, with the same crew. At least, that's my opinion.' Biggles tossed his cigarette end into the fire— 'And that, I'm afraid, is about as far as I can go in the matter of advice.'

The seaman drew a deep breath. 'Then it looks as if that's the end of it. I couldn't do a trip like that on my own.'

'And that's why you came to see me?'

'I thought we might do a deal.'

'Such as?'

'Well, I thought if you'd fix up a trip to fly there we could go shares in what we got. That would be fair enough, wouldn't it?'

'Certainly it would, if I could do it.' Biggles shook his head. 'But I'm afraid, Mr Grimes, putting the ownership of the gold on one side, the undertaking would be too big for me, even if I could get time off from my job to do it. I couldn't afford such an expedition as would be necessary — unless, of course, I was willing to take the most outrageous chances of losing my life, which I'm not. I don't mind reasonable risks, but I draw the line at suicide on the off-chance of getting a lump of gold, which may, or may not, be there.'

'Would it be as difficult as all that?' asked the sailor, in surprise. 'I mean, I thought aeroplanes could go pretty well anywhere.'

'A lot of people think that, and up to a point they are right,' agreed Biggles. 'But there are limits. Even though you've been to the Antarctic I don't think you quite realise what sort of place it is. We're talking about the most inaccessible place on earth. To go in a well-found ship would be a hazardous operation. To go in an aeroplane not properly equipped for the job would be asking for it. At least two planes would be needed, big planes — and aeroplanes are very expensive things.'

The sailor gazed at the floor. 'It didn't strike me as being as bad as all that.'

'Mebbe not, but you had firm planks under your feet. Let me try to make things a bit clearer. My business is flying, so I have to keep up to date with what's going on. Several Governments have an eye on the South Pole, and that's nothing to wonder at. You may say, why the South Pole more than the North? The answer is, the North Polar regions are mostly frozen seas, no use to anybody except as a meteorological station or military base. They were always easier to reach than the South Pole, which is land, a new continent, six million square miles of mighty mountain ranges without a living creature on them. The old scientists always asserted that as nearly all the known land masses are in the Northern Hemispheres, there must be a continent somewhere in the far south to balance them, otherwise the earth wouldn't rotate evenly on its axis. Well, the continent was there, although it took a bit of finding. They call it the White Continent, because it's in the grip of eternal ice and snow; but nobody knows what metals, coal and oil there may be in that ground for the first nation to tame it. Only one or two expeditions have seen it, but even they could hardly scratch the surface. The last expedition was American, and you can judge the sort of difficulties they expected by the size of the show. I won't bore you with the details, but these fellows had a rough time, although their planes were equipped with every modern appliance, regardless of cost. There were casualties, too, due to conditions outside all human knowledge or experience.'

'Such as?' asked Ginger curiously.

Biggles lit another cigarette. 'Apparently the first difficulty is to know where the water ends and the land begins. It's all a sheet of ice, and the outer edge of the ice-pack is always breaking off and floating away, so that the coastline is never the same. Consider landing. True, most of the ice is flat, but it is covered with finely-powdered snow about a foot deep. It never rains, of course, but it often snows, and when the wind blows it flings the snow about in swirling whirlpools, so that it's impossible to see the surface of the ice. It isn't only a matter of landing. If you get down you've got to get off again — some time. On fine days, apparently, you can get visibility up to a hundred and fifty miles in every direction, due to the absolute absence of humidity in the atmosphere. For the same reason the sky is purple, not blue, and although you get sub-zero temperatures the sun may burn the skin off you. If the weather clouds up, or you get a change of temperature, you get mist, and then you've had it. You get a phenomenon which the airmen of the last expedition called a white-out. You've heard of a black-out. Well, this is the same thing in reverse. Whichever way you look, up or down, it's always the same — just a white phantom world. The light comes from every direction, so there isn't even a shadow to help you. You can fly into the ground without even seeing it. Your altimeter is useless because you don't know the altitude of the ground below you. You may be flying over a plateau ten thousand feet high without knowing it. The mere thought of flying in such conditions is enough to give one a nervous breakdown. Navigation must be a nightmare. Remember, when you're at the South Pole, whichever way you face, you're looking north. You can't travel in any direction but north. Did you realise that? And if you happen to fly across the Pole, east immediately becomes west, and west, east. Silly, isn't it? I've never been, but I've read the reports of fellows who have, and if half of what they say is true I shan't burst into tears if I never see it. The nearest we've been is Kerguelen Island, and that's still a long way north of the Pole, but what with icebergs and fog, the going there wasn't exactly a joy ride. Well, I needn't say any more; I've said enough, I think, to make it clear that not even the most optimistic pilot would hardly expect to fly down to the *Starry Crown*, pick up the bullion and come home—just like that. I could get there, I've no doubt. It's the thought of getting stuck there that I don't like.'

'No, by Jove! I'm with you there, old boy,' put in Bertie, polishing his monocle.

'I see what you mean,' said Captain Grimes sadly.

'Of course, with time and unlimited money for equipment, there's no reason why the trip shouldn't be made; but you'll understand why I'm not keen to take a chance on my own account,' went on Biggles. He thought for a moment. 'There might be one way out of the difficulty,' he said pensively. 'The Government needs gold. Governments always do, but at this moment ours needs it more than ever before. If I put the thing up to them there's just a chance that they might sanction and finance an expedition, although in that case they'd want the gold, naturally. They might give us a rake-off — say, ten per cent — for our part in the undertaking. But even that would be better than a poke in the eye with a blunt stick. All we should have to lose then would be our lives. If you're agreeable, skipper, we could try it. The Government can only say no. If that's their answer, then as far as I'm concerned I'm afraid it's the end.'

'Aye, I'm agreeable,' answered the sailor. 'Will you do that?'

'I'll see about it right away,' promised Biggles.

Captain Grimes got up. 'All right, sir, let's leave it like that.'

Biggles, too, stood up. 'Very well. Leave me your address so that I can get in touch with you. If the trip comes off I'll make arrangements for both of you to come. I should need you, captain, anyhow, to guide us to the schooner. This boy of yours could act as mechanic and radio operator.'

'Right you are, sir. That's good enough for me,' decided Captain Grimes. 'Good day, sir.'

'Goodbye for now,' answered Biggles, seeing his visitors to the door.

'If this jaunt comes off, I shall need my winter woollies, by gad,' said Bertie.

'You certainly will, by gad,' returned Biggles grimly.

CHAPTER 3

SOUTHWARD BOUND

Fifteen days after the discussion in Biggles' London flat, a solitary, dark, airborne object moved southward above the Antarctic sea, grey, grim and forbidding in its sullen desolation. An air cadet would have recognised the aircraft for an elderly Wellington bomber, a type once the pride of the R.A.F., but now obsolete. In the cockpit sat Biggles and Ginger. Behind, in the radio compartment, sat ex-L.A.C. Grimes, now known for the purposes of the expedition as Grimy. With him was his father, Captain Grimes of the Mercantile Marine.

The fifteen days had been busy ones, for as soon as the flight had been sanctioned no time had been lost in its organisation. In fact, the trip had been launched, so Biggles asserted, much too quickly considering its hazardous nature; but this was unavoidable if the race against Lavinsky was to be won. Biggles had assumed that such a man would return to the polar sea. At any rate, he had accepted him as a factor to be reckoned with. If nothing was seen of him, so well and good. If a collision between the two parties did occur it was as well that they should be prepared. Biggles' great fear was that the man might get to the objective first. Every day's delay would increase that risk, for which reason not a minute had been wasted.

It had not taken Biggles long to decide on what he considered to be the best plan of campaign. Not that there had been much choice in the matter. The nearest

British territory to the objective — the only territory, in fact, within range of any available aircraft — was the Falkland Islands, the wild, rocky, windswept, treeless group which, lying three hundred miles south-east of the Magellan Strait, formed the southernmost colony of the British Empire. This, and the fact that frozen Graham Land, the objective, a thousand miles to the south, is a Dependency of the islands, made them the most obvious jumping-off place. As the islands were British there would be no difficulty about accommodation there, and the necessary arrangements were soon made between London and Port Stanley, the capital.

It is not to be supposed that the British Government Department responsible had accepted Biggles' proposal without question. Finance, as usual, was the chief stumbling-block; and it was not until Biggles pointed out that the cost of the trip would be relatively low compared with the profits should the raid be successful, that the expedition received official sanction. There had been a further snag when Biggles had demanded ten per cent of the value of any gold recovered, for distribution amongst those engaged in the enterprise. In this, however, Biggles had been adamant, stating that he was not prepared to risk his life, or the lives of his companions, from a mere spirit of adventure, of which he had had, and could still find, plenty, without going to the bottom of the world to look for it. In the end he had had his way, possibly because, as the authorities grudgingly admitted, he usually brought his undertakings to a successful conclusion. But a definite limit had been set to expenditure, following the usual official custom — as Biggles complained bitterly — of risking the ship for a ha'porth of tar. He had demanded two aircraft. Nothing, he stated, would induce him to even consider the trip with one. In this he also had his way, but he had to be satisfied with two obsolete Wellingtons from surplus war stores, which could, however, be modified to suit his requirements. Actually, they suited him well enough, for the machines were types of proved reliability. Reliability was the quality which interested him most, he said; reliability and range when loaded to capacity. Speed and height didn't matter.

The modifications presented no great difficulty. They consisted chiefly of extra tankage — for they would have to take all the fuel they needed with them — to give not only the necessary endurance range but a wide margin of safety. Heating equipment had to be installed. But the biggest alteration affected the landing chassis. This involved the fitting of skis over the wheels; that is to say, the fitment of skis in such a way that a few inches of tyre projected below them, in order that the machine could land on snow as well as on hard surfaces. This, he admitted, was not his own idea. The scheme had been tried and proved in practice by the last Antarctic air expedition. It was for this reason that he decided to adopt it. The machines, of course, were stripped of their armament and war gear. They would have plenty of weight to carry without these things.

The question of equipment had been fairly straightforward, for here again Biggles went to the trouble of studying the reports of previous expeditions, by sea as well as by air. It became a matter not so much of what to take, as what could be left behind, to limit the all-up weight, taking into consideration the extra fuel and oil. The planes would in any case be overloaded, as planes usually are on such occasions, but this would only affect the outward passage. Once at the objective everything could be unloaded, and if necessary left behind at the conclusion of the operation. Indeed, this would be inevitable if the gold was found, for it would have to be transported home. But, as Biggles observed, the first thing was to find the bullion. Once they had it stowed, everything else could be jettisoned for the thousand mile run back to the Falklands.

The first part of the outward trip, to the Falkland Islands, was a mere routine flight, permission of the intermediate countries having been sought, and obtained, by the Air Ministry. The two machines had flown in consort, crossed the Atlantic by the shortest route, from Dakar in West Africa to Natal in Brazil, and then followed the trunk route on down South America until it was necessary to turn east again on the final overseas leg to the Falklands. All this was a matter of simple navigation, and as the weather had been kind, no difficulties had been encountered.

At the Falklands they had received a cordial welcome from the Colonial Secretary, the British Naval Officer in charge, and the people; indeed, such hospitality were they shown that it became a problem for Biggles to convey, without divulging what they were doing, the urgency of their mission. It had been given out officially that they were on a survey flight, which up to a point was true enough; the difficulty was to reconcile this with Biggles' anxiety to be away. In the end he left the explanations to Algy and Bertie, who were now to remain behind as a reserve, and possible rescue party.

It was for this reason that Biggles had demanded two aircraft. By no means sure of what was likely to happen when they reached the objective he had jibbed at the idea of risking a landing which, should it go wrong, would leave them all marooned on the polar ice without the slightest hope of ever being picked up. The knowledge that a reserve machine was standing by to fetch them, should it be necessary, would make all the difference to their behaviour — not to say peace of mind. It was hoped that the two machines would always be in touch by radio, but should this arrangement break down it would be the task of the second machine to fly down to see what was wrong. As Biggles pointed out, if anything had gone wrong, if, for instance, the landing had been a failure, then those on the ground — or rather, on the ice — should be able to do something to prevent the second machine from making the same mistake. It should be possible for them to mark out a safe landing area, having cleared it of obstructions in the shape of projecting lumps of ice or soft snow. This was the plan. So far it had gone according to schedule. Algy and Bertie, with the reserve machine, were at Port Stanley. Biggles, Ginger, Captain Grimes and his son, after a day's rest, were heading south for the last known position of the long-lost schooner. Grimy, being a qualified radio operator, relieved Ginger of the necessity of remaining in the wireless compartment, while his father, who had seen something of the place from sea level, was to try to locate the schooner when they reached the area in which it had last been seen.

The day was fine, with visibility fairly good, but within an hour Ginger had realised the gravity of the business in which they were engaged. Already their lives were entirely dependent on the machine and its engines. Should these fail, then that would be the end, for in water of such a temperature as that below them life could not be maintained for more than a few minutes. These conditions were bound to have a psychological effect. It was not merely that they were out of sight of land that caused Ginger to regard the scene below and ahead with an unusual degree of apprehension, for that was nothing new. It was the knowledge of where they were far beyond the limits of any regular steamship route, that caused him to imagine sometimes that the engines had changed their note.

Far away to starboard he had watched the faint shadow that was the notorious Cape Horn, southern tip of the great American continent, fade away. He had looked at the chart on his knees. The very names of everything in the region were an unpleasant reminder of what they might expect to find a thousand miles farther on — Mount Misery, Desolation Island, Last Hope Bay, East and West Furies. These were the significant names bestowed by the early mariners. He wondered what names they would have found for the great southern continent, had they discovered it. But they had not. That had been left for a later generation of seamen. Even now, he pondered, the only visitor was an occasional whaler. The thought reminded him of Lavinsky. It would be odd, he thought, if they should see him. He scanned the desolate sea around but could see no sign of a ship. Ahead, all he could see was icebergs, like ghostly sentinels guarding the very end of the earth.

He looked at Biggles, but an expressionless face gave no indication of what he was thinking. Only his eyes moved from time to time, switching from the cold grey sea below to the instrument panel, and back again. Occasionally he made a note on a slip of paper. The aircraft droned on into the sullen emptiness.

Ice, big sinister bergs and smaller 'growlers', began to pass below. From the south came more and more, and ever more in endless succession. Some were white, some green, some blue, some weirdly luminous, some smeared with black stains as if they had been torn from the soil which no man had ever seen. Some towered high, like monstrous castles; others were flat plains on which an aircraft might land, or so it seemed. One he judged to be fully twenty miles long. It was a magnificent but soul-chilling spectacle, and there began to grow on him that feeling of human futility, when confronted by nature in the raw, that he had sometimes experienced when flying over the deserts of the Middle East. Yet even now, he brooded, the worst was yet to come.

For the first time he began to understand fully the dimensions of the task they had undertaken. Biggles, with his wide experience, had always realised it, of course. He had tried to make it clear when Captain Grimes had first come to see him. It would be hard, Biggles had said, to tell where the sea ended and the land began. It now became increasingly evident that they would not be able to tell. The large flat ice-fields were getting bigger as they neared the permanent pack-ice. Pieces, apparently, were always breaking off, pushed away by the eternal pressure from behind them. Areas of open water were getting smaller, and fewer. Presently, he perceived, there would be no water, only ice. What lay under it no man could say. It was getting colder, too, even in the heated cabin. The windows were beginning to fog up. At first he thought it was fog forming outside, but when he realised what was happening he took a rag and a bottle of alcohol, brought for the purpose, and wiped the perspex to prevent the condensation from freezing to opaque ice.

At last Biggles spoke. 'We're approaching the tip of Graham Land,' he remarked. 'It doesn't look much like land, does it? But if my navigation is correct, our time in air fixes our position. Confirm that Grimy is in touch with the base. He can give Algy our position and tell him I'm now going to alter course a trifle westerly. Ask Captain Grimes to come forward. I want to speak to him.'

Ginger went aft to obey the order, and presently returned with the information that contact had been maintained. The Skipper — as Captain Grimes was usually called — came with him.

'Take a look ahead, Skipper, and see if you can recognise anything,' requested Biggles. 'I fancy I can see rising ground. It looks like ice, but it may be a range of hills, in which case the thing should be permanent and serve as a landmark.' He passed his slip of paper. 'I make that to be our position. Your position when you spotted the wreck was about a hundred miles sou'-sou'-west of us. I'm now taking a course for it. I kept a little easterly at first because the Admiralty information is that the general drift of ice is north-east. I have made an allowance, therefore, for the wreck to move in that direction. If it has moved we should meet it.'

The Skipper subjected the region ahead to a long careful scrutiny. 'Can't say I recognise anything', he said at length. 'But there, I wouldn't expect to, because as the ice moves the scene changes.'

'Bound to,' agreed Biggles. 'What are our chances of spotting the wreck from up here, do you think?'

'Pretty poor, I should say, particularly if there has been snow since I last saw the place. The upper works of the *Starry Crown* are bound to be under snow, anyway.

Looking at her from sea level we could see her side, and the masts and standing gear stood out against the sky, even though they were iced up.'

'I'll drop off a little altitude as we go along,' decided Biggles. 'I'd rather not go below five hundred feet until I have to, for fear of hitting the tip of a big berg. Icebergs have an unpleasant habit of winding themselves up in a sort of invisible haze and then they're hard to see. You keep your eyes open for anything that looks like a ship, or anything else you saw the last time you were here.'

'Aye-aye.'

Ginger said nothing. If the truth must be told he was appalled by what he saw. To try to find a speck in such a waste — for that is all the ship would amount to — seemed hopeless. He hadn't realised until now that the *Starry Crown*, like everything else, would be white. He was not easily depressed, but had Biggles at that moment decided to turn his nose northward, he, for one, would have raised no objection.

Biggles, however, did not turn back. For rather more than half an hour he held his course, throttled back to cruising speed, down what he declared must be the western side of the Graham Peninsula, which thrusts a long arm northward as if pointing to South America. Beyond this there was no longer any open water. It had ended in a ragged line at a sheer wall of ice, which seemed to be anything from ten to a hundred feet high. Beyond this was only a white sameness, for the most part fairly level, but with occasional piled-up masses of ice, as if pressure from below had thrust it upwards. The rough waterline was the only guide, the one mark that was any use to them. Even this was not to be trusted, because the open water was strewn with floating fields of ice, large and small. But it did at least show the limit that a ship could reach. The Skipper, on the occasion of his last visit, must have passed just to the seaward of that line. At that time the hulk had been, according to his reckoning, between one and two miles inside the ice, locked fast in it.

Biggles began to circle, slowly losing height, following the line. He followed it for some distance, with floe-covered water to the north and sheer ice as far as the eye could see to the south. Nothing that remotely resembled a ship was seen. Once Ginger spotted and pointed out a number of huge, clumsy animals. The Skipper said they were Weddell seals, the only mammals that could live so far south. There were also big rookeries of penguins. A new menace appeared when the aircraft was suddenly surrounded by large, buff-coloured birds, with eagle-like beaks and black curved claws. The Skipper said they were skuas. For a minute or two there was some risk of collision; then the danger passed.

At last Biggles looked at Ginger and said: 'Well what are we going to do?'

'Are you asking me — seriously?' enquired Ginger in surprise.

'Yes. We've seen as much as we'll see from the air, so it's no use just using up fuel. If the hulk is still in existence it must be within twenty miles of the spot we're flying over now. She might be under a fresh fall of snow, in which case it's unlikely we'll see her. Our last hope is to land and look for her from ground level, but I'm not risking anybody's life by going down without his permission. It's for the rest of you to decide. Do we go down and set up camp, or do we go home.'

Ginger hesitated. The fact was, he was not happy about either plan, but the idea of going home empty-handed was the most repugnant. He shrugged. 'I'm in favour of going down. After all, it isn't as though we weren't prepared for a landing.'

'Suits me,' said the Skipper. 'I can speak for Grimy, too.'

'All right,' agreed Biggles. 'Go and tell Grimy to make a signal to base that we're going to land. Give him our position. You know where we are.'

'Aye-aye, sir.' The sailor went aft.

Biggles glided on to the nearest flat area. As far as space was concerned there was no difficulty. The surface was the big hazard, and that could only be ascertained by landing on it.

Ginger stared down as the machine skimmed low in a trial run. The surface looked perfect — hard, and as flat as a bowling green. He could see no obstruction. There was no wind, so the question of direction did not arise.

Biggles turned the aircraft and allowed it gently to lose height. He flattened out. Ginger held his breath. Nothing happened. Then his nerves twitched as the engines roared again and the machine swung up in a climbing turn.

Biggles laughed, a short laugh without any humour in it. 'See what I mean', he muttered. 'I thought I was on the carpet, but I must have flattened out about ten feet too high. Landing on snow is always tricky, but here, in this grey light, where there's nothing else but snow, it's definitely nasty.'

The next time, however, there was no mistake. There was a sudden vicious hiss as the skis touched. A cloud of fine, powdery snow, sprang high into the air, smothering the windscreen and blotting out the view. By the time it had cleared, as it quickly did, the machine was dragging, rather too quickly for comfort, to a standstill.

Ginger gave a heartfelt sigh of relief. He realised that without the skis the machine would have finished up on its nose.

Biggles looked at him and smiled. 'Well, here we are,' he said lightly. 'How does it feel to be on the bottom of the world?'

'Pretty chilly,' answered Ginger.

'It'll be colder still outside,' promised Biggles. 'Let's get down and see.'

CHAPTER 4

BEYOND MEN'S FOOTSTEPS

In two hours, clad in polar kit in a temperature that registered seventeen degrees below zero, a tent had been erected and well packed around with snow. In this, almost the entire load carried by the aircraft had been snugly stowed, leaving only enough space in the middle for the erection of a folding table. Around this packing cases had been arranged to serve as seats. Sleeping bags and blankets had been left in the cabin for the time being. It would, Biggles asserted, be warmer there.

No time had been lost in the unloading operation, Biggles being anxious to lighten the machine as quickly as possible to reduce the risk of the aircraft sinking into the powdery snow which, he was relieved to find, was only a few inches deep at the point on which he had chosen to land — about two hundred yards from the nearest open water. In this matter he may have been lucky, for there were places where the snow — tiny crystals, not unlike sugar — was much deeper. For this, apparently, the wind had been responsible. Little waves, like ripple sand, showed the direction of it.

They had this advantage, as Biggles reminded the others. There was no fear of darkness overtaking them, for the sun, at that particular period of the year, did not sink below the horizon, although it got very near to it. The result was, that every day was twenty-four hours of unbroken daylight. Nevertheless, at the normal period of night, the world was bathed in an eerie glow, through which the sun appeared as a monstrous red ball balanced on the distant ice.

From the aircraft, the landward side — if such an expression can be used — presented a fantastic picture. First, there was a gentle upward slope. Beyond this, ridges of ice, swept clear of the snow by wind, appeared as pale blue as grass-green hills. Some of these had castles and villages of ice piled on them, the illusion being strengthened by warm pink lights where facets of ice reflected the sun.

When everything was ship-shape a spirit stove was lighted and a meal prepared. It started with hot canned soup and finished with strong, sweet tea, the best stuff Biggles declared — and the Skipper agreed — for keeping the cold out.

'What do you think is our best way of trying to locate the hulk?' Biggles asked the Skipper, between mouthfuls of bread and jam.

'There's only one way to go about it that I can see, and that's to take walks out and back in every direction, like the spokes of a wheel, reckoning the camp to be the hub,' answered Captain Grimes. 'It's no use looking beyond the water line, because if the hulk ever got free she'd go down like a stone. Below her Plimsoll line she must have been crushed flat by the ice. That leaves us only half a circle to cover. We might walk a mile or two out, take a turn for about half a mile, and then come home again. In that way we ought to cover all the ground in a day or two. If we don't strike her we shall have to move camp and try again. It'll be hard going, but it's the only way.'

'What do you mean by hard going?' asked Ginger. 'It doesn't look too bad.'

'Wait till you try walking on the stuff and you'll see what I mean,' answered the Skipper. 'And I'm reckoning on the weather holding. It can change in a flash in this part of the world. The wind's only got to rise, or veer a point or two, and anything can happen. If it starts snowing —'

'Suppose we wait until it starts snowing before we talk about that,' broke in Biggles. 'No use jumping our fences until we come to them. We'll follow your advice about the walking. I can't think of anything better. You're sure this is the right place?'

'Must be, within a mile or two. It was a clear day when I took my position and there was nothing wrong with my instruments. I took care of that. I checked up three times, as I always do, so I don't see how I could go wrong. Of course, the ice may have moved, and the hulk with it. But we knew there was a risk of that before we started.'

As if to confirm this statement, from some distance away, on the seaward side, came a grinding, splintering clash, followed by a long, low growl.

'That's ice on the move now,' said Biggles. 'Sounded like two bergs bumping into each other.'

'Gives you an idea of what a hope a ship's got when she gets trapped between a couple of chunks like that,' put in the Skipper, grimly.

'Still, from our point of view the movement is very slow,' went on Biggles. 'According to the records of the scientists who have been here the big stuff only moves a matter of a few feet a day. I'm talking of the main pack, of course — the stuff we're on now. The smaller pieces that have broken off would move faster than that, no doubt, particularly with a wind behind them. If the hulk is here, or hereabouts, she couldn't have moved far since you last saw her.'

'She was fast enough in the ice then, and had been for many a year; so unless she's disintegrated she ought to be somewhere in the region now,' returned the Skipper. 'Of course,' he added, 'if her mast came down under the weight of ice, or anything like that, she'd be harder to see.'

Again from outside came the ominous growl of colliding ice.

'All right. The sooner we start looking for her, the better,' decided Biggles. 'I've seen all I want to see of the scenery, and I shouldn't sob my heart out if I never saw it again. Let's get cracking.' He got up.

'Are we all going to walk together?' asked Ginger.

Biggles considered the question. 'I don't think that's necessary,' he replied. 'I think the best plan would be for one to remain at home to act as cook, guard and signaller.. We'd look silly if we came back to find that a lot of seals had knocked everything to pieces.'

'What do you mean by signaller?' asked Ginger.

'Well, there's always the risk of fog or snow,' Biggles pointed out. 'If visibility happened to drop to zero it might not be easy for those who are out to find their way back to camp. In that case a pistol shot or two might save an awkward situation. The three walkers needn't stay together. They could walk a few hundred yards apart, always in sight of each other, so that visual signals could be made if need be.'

'That's the way to do it,' assented the Skipper. 'Safety first is the motto. You can't be too careful. I've heard of sealers getting lost within half a mile of their ship and never being seen again. It happened the very last time I was here. One of the hands was a Swede—a fellow named Larsen. Good sailor he was, too. At the last minute Lavinsky sent him back to fetch a sealskin that had been dropped. I reckon he chose him because he never did like him. Larsen didn't come back, and as the ice was closing in we went without him. Those were Lavinsky's orders, and I daren't go against the owners.'

'One would have thought,' said Ginger as he got ready, 'that nothing could have been more simple than a job like this, provided the machine always behaved itself. We knew exactly where we were coming and what we were going to do; but I've got an increasing feeling in my bones that we're up against something.'

'I never in my life heard of a salvage operation that went right from start to finish,' remarked Biggles. 'Something isn't where it should be, or something comes unstuck, somewhere, somehow. Read the records and you'll see that the unexpected is always turning up to make life harder for the people doing the job. But as I said before, we'll talk about the trouble when we bump into it.' Biggles looked seaward. 'All I have to add to that is, thank goodness we didn't come in a marine aircraft. I was tempted to choose a flying-boat, because, with water within range, landing would be a simple matter. When we arrived here there was enough open water in the offing for a fleet of battleships. Now look at it.'

Ginger looked, and saw that the water was almost entirely covered by small detached floes, each an island of ice. 'Had we landed out there in a flying-boat we should have been in a mess,' he observed. 'There isn't a run long enough anywhere to get a marine craft off. But, there, most of the ice seems to be floating away, so it might be all right.'

'And what would happen to a flying-boat in the meantime?' inquired Biggles cynically. 'One touch of that ice would rip her hull wide open. There's always a lot more ice under the water than there is showing. But that's enough talking. Let's go. Grimy, will you stay in camp to wash up and get supper? You'll have to melt snow for water. Skipper, will you take the first beat to the left, keeping as near to the water as is reasonably safe. If you see anything, give me a hail; I shall be next to you.'

'Aye, aye, sir.'

'Ginger, you take a half turn right,' went on Biggles. 'Don't get too wide. If you see any sign of a change in the weather give me a shout and make for home. Keep an eye on me for signals.'

'Good enough,' agreed Ginger.

'Okay, then. Let's get weaving.'

Each member of the party set off on his respective beat.

It did not take Ginger long to appreciate the truth of the Skipper's remark about the going being harder than it looked. It was much worse than he expected. He found it hard work, although this had an advantage in that it kept him warm. One thing that he was pleased to notice as he trudged on through the powdery snow: he left a trail so plain that there was no risk of losing it should he have to return by the same route.

As he tramped on, sometimes slipping on naked ice and often, ploughing through snow waist deep, the incongruity of what he was doing suddenly struck him. To look for an object the size of a ship in a snow-covered wilderness, where, he thought, a toy ship would have been conspicuous, seemed absurd. There was just a chance, he was bound to admit, that the ship might be behind one of the several masses of heaped-up ice that dotted the landscape, but the possibility of that seemed so remote as to be hardly worth consideration. The result was a feeling of hopelessness, of the futility of his task — a state of mind seldom conducive to success.

Away to his left, perhaps a quarter of a mile distant, was Biggles, as plain to see as a black beetle on a white carpet. Somewhere beyond him was the Skipper, also looking for a speck on a continent. Ginger could not see him, but he could watch Biggles. At least, he could see him for some time. When, presently, he disappeared, he assumed that either he was beyond the ridge or the higher ice towards which he had been walking. When several minutes passed and he had not reappeared, Ginger stopped, wondering if he ought to do something about it, and if so, what. He did not like to leave his beat; nor did he relish the idea of giving himself a longer march than was necessary, particularly as a slight breeze had sprung up, bitterly cold, to retard his movements. Happening to glance behind him, he noticed with a tinge of uneasiness that his trail, once so conspicuous, had disappeared; and he had not to look far for the reason. The snow was moving. At least, the surface was. The top inch or two seemed to be airborne, giving the surface a rough, blurred appearance. He was not worried about it. Visibility was still excellent; it did not appear to have disimproved in the slightest degree. Cupping his hands round his mouth he sent a hail across the waste. It had a strange, muffled sound. It was then that he noticed that he could no longer see the big pile of ice towards which Biggles had been marching. This was all the more odd because he could see the place where it had been — or he thought he could. Then, for the first time, a suspicion of the truth struck him. Swinging round he looked for the sun. It was not there. The whole length of the horizon was a dull uniform grey. That told him, beyond any shadow of doubt, that something was happening, although he was by no means sure what it was. Visibility still seemed good. But was it? Had it come to this, he wondered vaguely, that he could not believe his eyes? It seemed like it. He shouted again, and listened intently for an answer. None came. Turning about, he began to retrace his steps.

He had travelled, he thought, about two miles from camp. It had taken him rather more than an hour. He knew the direction of it, but all the same he was worried that the trail had been obliterated. Happening to glance behind him he was even more worried to see that his footprints were being filled in by whirling snow crystals almost as quickly as he made them. Feeling far from happy, he increased his pace.

It was soon evident that visibility was not so good as he had supposed, but he was still astonished that he could have been deceived so easily. Within half an hour he was struggling along through a vague world in which everything — ground, air and sky — seemed to be of the same uniform whiteness. These, he thought bitterly, were the very conditions that Biggles had been at pains to describe. He derived some satisfaction from the fact that he was on the ground, not in the air. The idea of flying in such conditions appalled him. But his exertions did at least keep him warm. Several times he thought he heard gunshots in the distance, but he could not be sure. The reports, if reports they were, and not icebergs in collision, were curiously flat and muffled. That, he soliloquised, might be due to the fog. He hoped it was so, for by now he should be nearer camp than the sounds suggested.

The crash of ice not far in front of him brought him to

an abrupt halt. He recognised the sound of ice floes in collision. Floating ice meant that he must be near open water. In that case, he thought swiftly, he must be near the camp — that is, if he had followed the true course home. Had he? He thought he had, but there was no means of confirming it. How could one be sure of anything in such conditions, he mused miserably. He walked on, slowly now, and soon saw that in one respect, at any rate, he had not been at fault. Before him the ice ended in a cliff some thirty feet high. Beyond it was the sea.

Stopping again he tried to reason the thing out. He now had a landmark — the open water. The camp was not far from it, but whether it lay to left or right he had no means of knowing. He shouted. He shouted again, and there was now a ring of anxiety in his voice. What really alarmed him more than anything was the absence of gunshots, for he felt certain that Grimy, perceiving what had happened, would be firing signal shots as arranged. He would hardly fail in the main reason for his being left in camp. So there Ginger stood, a prey now to gnawing indecision, knowing that if he moved, and the direction he took was the wrong one, he would only make his case worse.

In the end he made a plan. It was quite simple. He would follow the edge of the ice-cliff for a quarter of an hour by his watch. If, then, he could not locate the camp by shouting, he would retrace his steps for the same period of time, which would bring him back to the point on which he now stood. He would then do the same in the opposite direction. In this he felt fairly safe. There would be no risk of losing his way because he had the water to guide him. His mind made up, he set off.

His nerves, already at full stretch, suffered a jolt

when a great grey shape appeared suddenly out of the fog, gliding with a curious swinging motion towards him. Then he recognised it for a Weddell seal. He had seen these creatures from the air without realising they were so big. The animal stopped dead when it saw what was, perhaps, the first human being it had ever seen. Ginger also stopped. Apparently the surprise was mutual. Then the animal, with a grunt, continued on its way without taking further notice of the intruder. It passed within a few yards of where Ginger stood, reached the rim of the ice, made a spectacular dive, and was seen no more.

Ginger's adventure ended in a rather ridiculous anticlimax. The haze began to clear as quickly as it had formed. Suddenly, to his joy, he heard voices. He let out a yell. It was answered at once. He walked on towards the sound, and presently the familiar shape of the tent loomed before him. Standing in front of the entrance were the rest of the party.

'Where have you been?' inquired Biggles.

'Where have I been?' Ginger was astonished by the question. 'I've been lost,' he announced curtly.

'Lost! Where?'

'In the fog?'

'What fog?'

'Are you kidding?' demanded Ginger suspiciously.

'No.'

'Didn't you see any fog?'

'There was a little thin mist but nothing to speak of,' returned Biggles. 'I lost sight of you, but I wasn't worried. I waved to the Skipper and we came home.'

'Well, where I was the fog was as thick as pea soup,' declared Ginger. 'I couldn't see a thing.'

'Curious,' replied Biggles. 'You must have struck a

peculiar slant of air. I seem to remember reading something about the fog here often being patchy and quite local.'

'Patchy or not, it had me worried,' asserted Ginger, feeling somehow that he had been cheated. He looked at Grimy. 'I listened for signal shots.'

'There didn't seem any need,' answered Grimy. 'I could see the others coming so I guessed you wouldn't be far away.'

'You're quite right — I wasn't,' confirmed Ginger. 'My trouble was I didn't know it.'

'Did you see anything looking like a ship?' asked Biggles.

'Not a sign. Did you?'

Biggles shook his head. 'No, neither did the Skipper. All I saw was snow, and there was plenty of that.'

'If we ever find this ship I'll be ready to believe anything in the future,' stated Ginger.

'We'll try again to-morrow,' said Biggles. 'Come and have something to eat.'

CHAPTER 5

INTO THE PAST

For three anxious, rather boring days, the search for the castaway schooner continued along the lines planned, but without the slightest encouragement. No one said anything, but each knew what the others were thinking. Long silences made it clear that hopes were fading. Anything like enthusiasm had certainly been extinguished. Eager anticipation had become mere labour. What was to have been a treasure hunt had become a tiresome task to be performed. However, no one had as yet mentioned failure.

At intervals, two or three times a day, Biggles ran up the engines to keep them in working order. So far, the frost had not affected them. He was concerned mostly with the lubrication system, but it seemed to be all right. For the rest, the long Antarctic days continued without incident and without any appreciable change in the weather. From the direction of the open water came the growling and muttering of icebergs waging ceaseless war with each other.

For one thing the party was particularly thankful. Visibility after the first day had remained good. Not that there was much risk now of any member of the party losing his way. After Ginger's early experience Biggles had seen to that by the simple expedient of knocking some packing cases to pieces and slicing the wood into long, thin splinters. Anyone leaving camp took a bundle of these with him, sticking one into the snow at intervals on the outward journey and recovering them on the way back. By this means, not only could a man be sure of finding his way home, but in the event of accident there would be no difficulty in trailing a searcher who failed to return.

Four-fifths of the ground to be surveyed had now been covered. All these had yielded was the sight of an endless wilderness of snow, with mountains, also snow-clad, in the far distance. One segment remained. If it produced no result, Biggles had said, then the site of the camp would have to be shifted a few miles to the east, this being the direction of the general ice-drift according to scientific investigation. The whole process would then be repeated, subject to the weather remaining fair. When the machine was in the air, making the move, Algy and Bertie could be given the new position.

Everyone was disappointed by the failure, so far, of the mission, the Skipper most of all, for he insisted on shouldering responsibility. His early confidence that he could not have made a mistake when working out his ship's position, on the occasion of his previous visit, was being shaken. Biggles admitted that the present circumstances were not exactly encouraging, but asserted that they were still far from being beaten. They were all fit, not even tired. The cold, dry atmosphere was exhilarating, and it had all been very interesting, anyway. They had seen what few mortal eyes had been privileged to see, even though the landscape was nothing to rave about.

On the morning of the fourth day the final search from the existing camp began. The party consisted of the Skipper, Grimy and Ginger, it being Biggles' turn to act as camp orderly. The Skipper took the left-hand beat. Ginger was on the extreme right, which meant that he would have to march almost due west, keeping roughly parallel with the irregular ice cliff that fringed the open water.

He set off on what had become almost a routine operation. Every hundred yards or so he pulled a stick from his bundle and planted it in the snow, leaving about eighteen inches exposed. Progress, he found, was slower than it had ever been before. This was due to several causes. In the first place, he had to more or less follow the ice-and-water line. This was as irregular as the edge of an unfinished jig-saw puzzle. Naturally, this meant that he had much farther to go than if he had followed a straight course. Again, near the water, although this had not been apparent from the camp, the ice was far from flat. Either from pressure behind, or below, it had been lifted into long, frozen corrugations. In extreme cases the ridges had burst upwards in piles of ice of every shape known to geometry. This hid what lay ahead, and as more and more ice fell away behind him his view to the camp was cut off. Otherwise he would have seen it, for while the sky was grey, with a layer of high cloud, visibility on the whole was good. So with one thing and another the going was hard, and he was soon perspiring freely. But there was this about it, he thought, as he struggled on towards more broken ice: here it would be easily possible for an object even the size of a ship to remain unobserved except from close range. Against that, however, was the fact that he was much nearer to the sea than the hulk had been when it was last sighted. At that time, according to the Skipper, it had been at least a mile inshore, whereas now he was seldom more than a hundred yards from the water. Still, he did not lose sight of the possibility of some of the ice-cliff breaking away, which would have the effect of bringing the hulk nearer to the sea.

After passing across a broad field of snow he was approaching one of the big malformations of ice, when, just short of it, he struck his knee against a piece that he had not noticed. This was not an uncommon occurrence, as, owing to the absence of shadows and the resulting white flatness, small objects blended easily into the background. Muttering in his annoyance he stooped to rub his knee, for he had given it a sharp blow, although the thick stockings he wore prevented an actual wound. In stooping, he noticed something which at first did no more than arouse his curiosity. He was accustomed to seeing ice of peculiar shapes, but the piece into which he had blundered was very odd indeed. First, there was a low symmetrical mound. From this, for no reason which he could discover, rose a quite definite cross. As white as the surrounding snow, in a churchyard it would have been commonplace; but here, a thousand miles from the nearest church, he could only regard it with amazement. He stopped rubbing to stare at it. A cross! A distant bell rang in his memory. Quite recently somebody, somewhere, had said something about a cross, something, he thought, in connection with what they were doing. Then he remembered. One of the men concerned with the story of the *Starry Crown* — he could not remember his name — had killed his companion, built a cairn over his body and topped the edifice with a cross. Doubtless other men had died on the ice, to be buried by their shipmates. Was this one of them, or was it the man who had died near the schooner. He would soon see.

With pulses now beating fast he took out his heavy hunting knife and opening the biggest blade struck the point into the ice. A chip flew off. He struck again and again, causing the ice, as brittle as glass, to fly in all directions. In a couple of minutes he had reached what he hoped to see, and for that matter, what he fully expected to see. Wood. The ice was not solid. It had formed a crust over a wooden object, and from its shape that object could only be a cross. He began working on the crossbar, knowing that if there was any writing it would be here. It was. In five minutes more the board was exposed sufficiently for him to read a rough inscription, incised, it seemed, with the hard point of a lead pencil. It read:

JOHN MANTON

DIED 1877

R.I.P.

'Rest in peace,' breathed Ginger. Well, Manton had certainly done that. Straightening his back Ginger wiped his forehead with the back of a hand which now trembled slightly as his imagination ran riot. Here, then, at his feet, in loneliness utter and complete, lay the body, preserved in the eternal ice, of the man who had set out to do the very thing that he himself was now doing. Manton had come for gold. He had stayed, and would stay, for ever and ever — unless the earth moved on its axis, which did not seem likely.

Ginger shivered, glancing around apprehensively. The air seemed to have turned a shade colder. Then his imagination took a more material turn. Manton, he recalled, had been killed by the man Last. That final tragedy of solitude had occurred in or near the schooner. Last would not have carried the body of his victim far. There was no need. It followed, therefore, that the schooner was near at hand — or had been. If it was near, why hadn't he seen it? He gazed around, his eyes travelling slowly over the scene of Last's ghastly ordeal. He could picture him wild-eyed and horror stricken, dragging the corpse of his one solitary companion to the very spot on which he now stood. It was easier here, than at home, to feel the full force of that terrible moment. No wonder Last had faced the open sea in a cockleshell boat rather than leave his bones beside those of the friend whose life he had taken.

Ginger's eyes moved to the tumbled mass of ice towards which he had been walking when he had struck his knee. At first, it still seemed shapeless; so much so that had he not collided with the cross he knew that he would have walked past it without a second glance. But now, as he stared at it, with the help of a little imagination the mass began to take form. Without much effort he could make out the rough shape of a ship's hull. With a little more effort he could locate the superstructure. But where were the masts on which they had reckoned to reveal the ship's position. Certainly they were not there — at any rate, not where they should have been. Then, staring hard, he understood. Right across the deck stretched a line of ice so straight that it was hard to suppose that it could have been formed without a foundation. Ginger realised that this must be the mast; but it had fallen, and in its new position had soon collected a coating of ice and snow. From it, projecting downwards in rigid lines, were what had once been supple ropes.

For a moment or two Ginger stood still. The knowledge that he had found what, in his heart, he had never expected to see, set in motion a strange feeling of unreality. His knees went curiously weak and he found himself trembling. What was it about gold, he wondered vaguely, that affected men in such a way? But was he counting his triumph too soon? Was the gold still there? Should he return at once to report his discovery to Biggles or should he first confirm that they had not been forestalled by another treasure seeker? If he went back to camp to report that he had found the ship, the first thing everyone would want to know, would be, was the gold still there? The hulk, without it, was nothing. The gold was everything. So ran his thoughts.

It did not take him long to reach a decision. He would have a look inside the hulk, anyway, if only to confirm that it was the ship they were looking for. It should not take long.

He had some difficulty in getting on the sloping deck — or what had once been a deck, for now, of course, it was under a layer of ice of unknown thickness. He slid off several times. But in stumbling around, looking for an easier place, he came upon something that exceeded his hopes. It was a narrow flight of steps cut in the ice, so regular that it could only have been made by human hands.

Having gained the deck he again looked about him for some way of getting inside the hulk, and he was not altogether surprised to see that from the steps he had mounted there appeared to be a track leading to a hump of ice that must have been the cover of the companionway. He was not surprised because he remembered that he was not the first visitor to the ship after it had become ice-bound. Men had lived there for months. Naturally, they would be constantly going up and down. Walking on he saw that his surmise was correct. A hole had been cut in the ice, in the manner of a cave. Looking in he saw ice-encrusted steps leading downwards, although in his amazement at the sight that met his gaze he hardly noticed them. The place was a grotto, far exceeding in sheer fantasy those commonly pictured in books of fairy tales.

His wonderment increased as he picked a cautious way down the slippery steps and presently stood inside the ship. Here the picture presented transcended all imagination. Light and ice together made play in a manner no artist could hope to portray. Everything was ice, taking the shape of the object on which it had formed. Where the light actually came from was not easy to see, but Ginger could only assume that it came from above, where the deck had been crushed and punctured by the weight of ice on it. Through the ice that covered such gaps the light filtered, and the result was an eerie luminosity. Even the very atmosphere seemed tinged with unearthly hues never seen by human eyes. The roof and walls, floodlit by beams of daylight passing through pure ice, were sheer crystal. From the ceiling hung sparkling chandeliers ablaze with prismatic jewellery. From clusters of diamonds long pendants of precious stones hung down, in one place rubies, in another emeralds, and in another sapphires. In such entrancing surroundings, for a little while Ginger could only stand and stare, unconscious of the passing of time, unconscious of everything except an increased feeling of unreality. Then, slowly, he made his way into the fairy ice palace, following a corridor that seemed to run the full length of it.

In the first room he entered another surprise awaited him. It was, apparently, the compartment that had been used as a mess room by the wretched men who had found themselves prisoners in this world of ice. Crocks and cutlery lay about as if they might have been used that very day. There was food, too, on plates and in opened tins. He picked up a biscuit on which unknown hands had placed a slice of bully beef, and smelt it. It was quite fresh and sweet. There was, after all, nothing remarkable about that, he mused. The ship was a natural refrigerator in which food would keep for ever. Corruption does not begin below freezing point.

He walked on, looking into several cabins. The doors all stood wide open. But he saw nothing of particular interest. In one lay a pile of blankets, as if thrown aside by a man who had just slept there. The end room, however, was larger than the rest. Not only were the walls jewel-encrusted but on the far side the ice, as if melted by heat, had run down to form columns, row after row of luminous pipes in the manner of a church organ. To this weird phenomenon, however, Ginger paid little attention. His eyes were focused on the middle of the room, where stood a large deal table — or rather, he stared at what was on it. It was a stack of bars, all the same shape and size. They were black. He was disappointed that they were not yellow, for then he would have known that his quest had ended.

Stepping closer to the table he reached for one of the bars to examine it; but when he went to pick it up he was amazed by its weight. In fact, he could not lift it. He could only drag it towards him. Could this be—? His heart began to thump. He reached quickly for his knife. One snick in the side of a bar told him all he needed to know. The cut metal gleamed, and the colour was yellow. He knew then that he had found the gold. He had found it! It was only self-consciousness that prevented him from shouting.

It was at this moment, while he stood gazing

fascinated at the stacked bars before him, that he thought he heard a sound. It was very slight, a faint crunch, as if a piece of ice had been crushed. He paid little attention to it, however, supposing that such sounds in such a place were only to be expected. All the ice around him was constantly subject to pressure. Then an idea struck him, one that pleased him greatly. He would take a piece of the gold back with him. He couldn't carry an entire bar. That was out of the question. But gold, pure gold, he recalled, had the quality of being soft, so that he should have no difficulty in cutting off a piece with his knife. He would take it back to camp and enjoy the expressions on the faces of his friends when they realised what it was. Making a rough measurement with his knife he started sawing at the end of the bar that lay nearest, smiling to himself at the thought that few people had a chance to saw up pure gold.

The smile died suddenly as, while thus engaged, he heard another sound. This time there was nothing natural about it, and he was definitely startled. It sounded like what is usually called a chuckle — the soft sound made by a human being who is quietly amused. Ginger stopped sawing and stood tense, while cold fingers seemed to touch the back of his neck and slide down his spine. He was not superstitious, but he remembered where he was, and the horrors that had been enacted in that very room. Perhaps the very fingers that had last touched that bar of gold were now frozen in death in the ice just outside. Could it be possible that Manton's spirit, unable to rest — He looked around furtively. Nothing moved. The silence was profound.

He tried to persuade himself that the noise had been

made by a cruising skua, although in his heart he knew that the noise was utterly unlike that made by any bird. Yet, he thought, the skua was an exceptional bird to live in such inhospitable surroundings. Telling himself not to be a fool he again turned to his task, but he had not even begun when he saw, or thought he saw, a shadow flit acoss the room — exactly where, he couldn't say, although it seemed as if something solid had passed between the light and the pipes of the ice-organ. Could it have been the shadow of a cloud, passing across the face of the sun? But there was no sun. The sky was grey. Again he experienced the feeling of an icy hand creeping down his back. He could not deceive himself. Something, somewhere, had moved. Could it have been his own shadow? It might have been. Calling himself a child for being frightened by his own shadow he tried to laugh it off, but it was a poor effort. His nerves were going to pieces, and he knew it. He would finish the job quickly, and go. That he might not be alone in the ship was still something that did not occur to him, and for this, in the circumstances, he was hardly to be blamed.

He turned back to the bar, but found it impossible to concentrate on what he was doing. His gaze seemed drawn irresistibly to the far side of the room, to the organ, where the shadow had stopped. His eyes wandered over it. They halted abruptly, and remained fixed, staring at something that stared back at him through a hole in the ice. It was an eye. He could see it distinctly; a human eye it appeared to be, for surrounding it was the small part of a dead white face. It did not move, but it glowed, as if imbued by inhuman fire.

CHAPTER 6

GINGER RUNS AWAY

We have already said that Ginger was not superstitious. His life had lain along lines too materialistic for that. Nor was he easily frightened. He had looked Old Man Death in the face too often. But death was something he understood. What he now saw was something he did not understand, and to say merely that he was frightened would be to say nothing at all. He was, literally, paralyzed by fright. Perhaps for the first time he comprehended fully the meaning of the word fear — the fear that comes from something beyond human understanding. He was not conscious of this. If he was conscious of anything it was an overwhelming sensation of sheer horror, a nameless dread that gripped his tongue, dried his mouth to the dryness of ashes and turned his muscles to water. He could not turn his eyes away from the awful Thing, but stood rigid, as if mesmerised. The eye, unwinking, stared back.

How long he stood there, staring, with his heart beating on his eardrums, he never knew. He forgot all about the gold. It might not have existed. He forgot everything. But in human existence everything has an end, and thus with Ginger's temporary petrification. Fear was succeeded suddenly by panic, and panic has the quality of being mobile. So to Ginger returned the power of movement, and when it came it came with a rush. An inarticulate cry burst from his lips, and, turning, he fled. Out of the dreadful chamber, straight down the passage he tore in a shower of ice-gems detached by the vibration of his flying footsteps, certain that something frightful was at his heels. He took the companion steps in three jumps, skidded across the glassy deck, and in another reckless bound reached the level ice. Nor did he stop there. On he sped, to fall with a crash as he collided full tilt with Manton's ice tombstone. He had forgotten it. He did not see it. He did not stop to pick it up. He had taken a brutal fall, for the ice was hard; but he felt no pain. Gasping, he scrambled madly to his feet and raced on. At that moment he had one idea in life, one only; and that was to put as wide a distance between himself and the haunted ship as was possible in the shortest space of time.

Once clear, he risked a glance behind, but seeing nothing, some degree of sanity returned. Panting, he steadied his pace, and not until then did he become aware that it was snowing. That sobered him. Fortunately he had not gone far, and casting about, soon came upon one of his guide-sticks. That went far to restore him, for he knew that without it he would have been lost indeed. Apparently the snow had just started, and as there was no wind he could discern faintly the trail his feet had made on the outward journey. He followed it at a run. The crash and crunch of distant bergs formed a fitting accompaniment to his shattered nerves. The snow, after all, turned out to be only a shower, and slowly died away to a fairly clean but leaden calm.

When he came in sight of the camp he saw that the others were all home. All were engaged in clearing the new snow from the upper surfaces of the aircraft, a task they had almost completed. When they saw him coming they desisted and returned to the tent, there to await his arrival

It can hardly be said that Ginger arrived back in camp. He tumbled into it, spent and shaken. Almost sobbing from reaction he sank down on the nearest packing case and buried an ashen face in trembling hands.

The others gathered round, looking from one to another.

Biggles was the first to speak. 'What's the matter with you,' he asked sharply.

Ginger drew a shuddering breath and looked up. 'I'm sorry — but — I can't help it,' he blurted.

'Can't help what?'

'Being like this. I'm all to pieces. I feel awful.'

'What happened?'

'I — I don't really know,' stated Ginger. 'It must seem silly to you, but nothing like this has ever happened to me before. I've seen — a ghost.'

'You've seen *what*?'

'A ghost.'

Biggles made a sign to the Skipper: 'Get me the brandy flask out of the medicine chest,' he ordered curtly. 'I don't know what's happened but he's suffering from shock — pretty severe shock, too. Grimy, get a blanket and throw it over his shoulders, then put some milk on the stove.'

The Skipper brought the flask, poured a little of the brandy into a cup and passed it to Biggles, who thrust it at Ginger. 'Drink this,' he ordered crisply.

The cup rattled against Ginger's teeth as he complied, spluttering as the potent spirit stung his throat. Without a word he handed the cup back to Biggles and wiped away the tears that the unaccustomed liquid had brought to his eyes.

'Now, what's all this about?' demanded Biggles. 'Pull yourself together.'

Ginger drew a deep breath and held out his trembling hands. 'Look at me,' he said weakly. 'I didn't get like this for nothing.'

'I can believe that,' answered Biggles. 'What caused it?'

'I don't rightly know,' admitted Ginger. 'I wasn't so bad until I saw the eye.'

Biggles frowned, looking hard at the speaker. 'Eye! What eye? Whose eye?'

'I don't know.'

Biggles caught Ginger by the shoulders and shook him. 'Snap out of it,' he ordered. 'So you saw an eye. Okay. Where was it?'

'In the ship.'

'Ship! What Ship?'

'The *Starry Crown.*'

Dead silence greeted this announcement. Then Biggles went on, speaking slowly and deliberately. 'Are you telling us that you have found the *Starry Crown*?'

'Yes.'

'Where?'

Ginger pointed. 'Somewhere over there, about three miles for a guess.'

Biggles made a sign to the others to be patient. By this time he had realised that Ginger had had such a shock, real or imaginary, that comes only once in a lifetime. 'Go on,' he invited. 'Take your time. We're in no hurry. So you found the ship. What next?'

As the brandy took effect Ginger began to feel better. He became more coherent. 'First of all I found the grave,' he explained.

'Whose grave?'

'Manton's. The cross Last put up is still there. I cut away the ice and saw the name. Then I knew the ship must be somewhere near. I found it, all covered in ice. It wasn't easy to see. I went aboard to see if the gold was still there.'

'Was it?'

'Oh yes. It's there all right.'

'Did you actually touch it?'

Ginger stared. 'What do you mean — touch it?'

'I mean — you didn't dream it.'

'Dream it my foot,' cried Ginger hotly. 'I was hacking off a lump to bring home to show you.'

'Why didn't you?'

'That's what I'm trying to tell you,' protested Ginger. 'While I was sawing away I heard a movement. I didn't take much notice of it at the time. Then I heard someone chuckle — horrible.'

'And then you bolted?'

'I did not,' asserted Ginger. 'I wasn't feeling too happy, I'll admit, remembering that a dead man was lying just outside; but I went on with what I was doing. But looking up I caught sight of an eye watching me.'

'So what?'

Ginger shrugged 'That finished me — and it would have finished anybody.' Ginger frowned at the scepticism on Biggles' face. 'Don't you believe me?'

'Well, you must admit it sounds a pretty tall story,' returned Biggles. 'But even if we take your word for it that all this really happened, what does it add up to. You heard a sound, and then you saw an eye looking at you. What's odd about that? You've seen an eye before to-day.'

'Not like this one,' said Ginger warmly.

'Was there only one eye?'

'I could only see one.'

'Are you trying to say you saw an eye wandering about without a face?'

'There was a little piece of face. The skin was white—a sort of dirty fish-belly white.'

Biggles lit a cigarette and flicked the match away. 'Did you by any chance have a fall and bump your head before you found the ship?'

'Are you suggesting I knocked myself silly and imagined this?' cried Ginger hotly.

'I wondered—'

'Well, you needn't,' declared Ginger vehemently. 'I found the ship, I tell you. Aladdin's cave was nothing to it. It was marvellous, all rainbows and coloured lights, jewels—'

'Now, wait a minute,' interrupted Biggles gently. 'It sounds to me as if you've got this ship all mixed up with the neon lights in Piccadilly on a fine night.'

'All right,' said Ginger wearily. 'Have it your own way. I'm telling you what I saw. I was as right as rain until that eye squinted at me.'

'Where exactly was it?'

'Behind a sort of curtain of ice at the far end of the room.'

'Didn't it move?'

'No.'

'Then why get in such a sweat about it? Didn't you go up to it to make sure it wasn't just another piece of ice with the light shining through it?'

'I certainly did not,' answered Ginger coldy. 'That was the *last* thing that occurred to me.'

'What did you do?'

'I ran—and when I say I ran I mean I didn't dawdle

to examine the icicles on the way. No, sir. I was out of the ship so fast that a bullet coming behind me would have been left standing. My jump from the deck to the ice would be a world record if it could be measured. I nearly knocked myself out falling over Manton's grave. I took an awful tumble, and it was only the thought of the dead man under me, and the eye behind me, that got me on my feet again. It was some time before I realised it was snowing. That should give you an idea of the state I was in. I didn't stop running all the way home. Look at me. My nerves are pulp. It takes more than imagination to do that.'

'Imagination can play queer tricks,' remarked Biggles quietly. 'The result can be the same as reality, perhaps worse; but I must admit that when you arrived here you looked more like a corpse than a live explorer.'

'You see, the trouble was, I wasn't expecting to find anyone else on the ship,' explained Ginger.

'I can believe that,' replied Biggles. 'It wouldn't be the sort of place you'd expect to find a picnic in progress. However, I'll believe in this floating eye when I see it.'

'I tell you, there's something, or somebody, in that ship,' expostulated Ginger sullenly.

'Well, it should be fairly easy to confirm that,' retorted Biggles. 'I'm not really inquisitive by nature, but I must confess that I'm all agog to have a look at this remarkable eye. Would you mind coming back and showing it to me?'

'What — me?' cried Ginger, rising in alarm. 'Go back to that ship? Not on your life — not if she was stuffed with diamonds as big as footballs. I shall see that accursed eye leering at me for the rest of my days. I won't even dare to sleep for fear it haunts my dreams.'

'Okay — okay!' said Biggles impatiently. 'Will you take us as far as the ship. If you'll show it to me I'll guarantee to gouge out this disconcerting optic.'

Ginger hesitated. 'All right. I wouldn't mind doing that — but I shall take a gun.'

'Good enough. You can take a battery of howitzers as far as I'm concerned; but somehow I don't think you'll need anything like that. I suppose you'll be able to find your way back?'

'Easily. I left my sticks in. I came home in too much of a hurry to pull them out.'

'I see,' said Biggles. 'We'll just have a cup of tea while you're catching up with yourself, then we'll go and collect the bullion.'

CHAPTER 7

THE HORROR IN THE HULK

It was late in the evening although, of course, it was still light, when Biggles, Ginger and the Skipper set off to investigate the mystery. Grimy had been left behind as camp guard and mess orderly. As a matter of detail, Ginger, who was still not quite himself, had suggested that the trip be postponed until the following day, but Biggles was opposed to the delay, saying that he did not like the look of the weather. This was not to be disputed, for the sun, a gigantic crimson ball hanging low over the horizon, could only just be seen through a haze. The sky overhead seemed reasonably clear, but the Skipper agreed that there was a suspicion of more snow in the air. A rising temperature also threatened fog. Biggles maintained that if they did not go at once they might never go, for if the weather deteriorated it would be madness to stay on the ice at all.

If the gold was really there, then they would carry straight on, taking it out of the ship and putting it into a position from where it could easily be picked up, Biggles had said. They would then radio for Algy, and with the gold stowed in the two machines, make for home. Ginger had protested at Biggles use of the word 'if,' which implied that he was still sceptical about the gold. Biggles had admitted frankly that he was. Had Ginger merely said he found the gold, he, Biggles, would have taken his word for it without question; but if Ginger's nerves were in such a state that he imagined he had seen a ghost, which was absurd, he might also have imagined that he had seen the gold. Ginger saw that argument was useless. He saw, too, that if the eye had vanished, or if it turned out to be an illusion created by a freak of the ice, he would look a fool, and it would take him a long time to live the business down. Secretly he hoped it would still be there; but even he was beginning to wonder if he had made a mistake. The long-abandoned ship was an eerie place, and his nerves *had* been at full stretch, he reflected.

A steady tramp of just over an hour brought the party to within sight of the mass of ice which, Ginger claimed, held in its cold embrace the remains of the doomed vessel. Biggles' scepticism as he stared at it increased rather than diminished. From a distance, at any rate, it required a big effort of the imagination to discern the shape of a ship in the formless pile of blue-and-white ice. Ginger admitted this. It was likely, he said, that he would have walked past the ice without another glance, had it not been for the cross.

But when the cross was reached, lying where it had fallen, and Ginger displayed triumphantly the name of the dead mariner on the cross-bar, Biggles' expression changed. He looked at it and then gazed long and steadily at the chaos of ice. 'By thunder! I believe he's right,' he acknowledged in a curious voice.

'Well, there it is. What are you going to do about it?' inquired Ginger, trying to speak calmly.

'For a start I'm going to winkle out this eye that seems to have put the fear of the devil into you,' answered Biggles.

'Now, you listen to me,' said Ginger, with unusual earnestness. 'Be careful. There's somebody in that ship. I began to doubt it myself as we walked along, but now

I'm back I'm sure of it. I can feel it in my bones.'

'Don't talk nonsense,' snapped Biggles. 'If there's an eye there's a human being, and that's something I can't believe. It doesn't make sense. And, anyhow, even if by some incredible chance there was a man in the ship, why should he stand still and squint at you? Surely he would have shouted with joy at seeing a deliverer.'

Ginger shrugged. 'All right. Have it your own way. I can't explain the thing any more than you can. But let me ask you this: Have you ever before seen me in such a mortal funk?'

'No, I can't say I have,'

'Then what caused it? It must have been *something*.'

'Yes, I suppose it must,' admitted Biggles. 'But standing here won't solve the mystery. We'll soon settle the matter.'

'Okay. Go ahead — but watch your step,' replied Ginger. 'Don't say I didn't warn you.'

Biggles smiled. 'I won't,' he promised.

The party advanced, Biggles leading, Ginger bringing up the rear. He pointed out the ice steps by which he had reached the companion-way. Biggles did not answer, but when they were all on the deck he turned. 'Stand fast,' he said, and then went on alone to the hole in the ice that gave access to the companion-steps and the lower deck. He looked inside and let out a low whistle. 'I must say it's all very pretty-pretty,' he told Ginger, in a glance over his shoulder. Turning again he shouted, 'Hi! Anyone there?'

There was no answer, but a moment later a movement farther along the deck caught Ginger's eye. Turning quicky he was just in time to see a dark object, the size of a football, where a moment before he would have sworn there had been nothing. Staring, he made it out to be a head, human, yet scarcely human. All that could be seen clearly was the middle part of the face, for above and below was a matted crop of reddish hair. Then it was gone.

Had Ginger been able to move he knew he would have run for his life; but all he could do was let out a strangled shout.

Biggles, who was just entering the companion, looked back. 'Now what is it?' he asked irritably.

Ginger gulped. 'A head,' he managed to get out. 'A head, all hair and beard.'

Biggles stared incredulously. 'Where?'

Ginger pointed.

Biggles looked. 'I can't see anything.'

'It's gone.'

Biggles looked again at Ginger. 'So now the eye has found a face to live in,' he scoffed. 'What's the matter with you? You don't usually behave like this.'

'Things like this don't usually happen,' answered Ginger weakly. 'Come on. Let's get out of this.'

'Oh, for the love of Mike pull yourself together,' requested Biggles impatiently. As he finished speaking he turned back to the companion. 'Anyone there?' he called loudly. But in spite of the question it was obvious from his manner that he did not expect an answer. Nor for the moment was there one. He took a step forward, then, suddenly, he flung himself aside with such speed that he slipped and fell. But any amusement this may have caused died at birth when the reason for the quick move revealed itself. Out through the opening flew an axe. It struck the frozen rigging with a crash and brought down a load of icicles.

By the time the noise of this had died away Biggles was on his feet, with such an expression on his face as

Ginger had never seen before. No longer was he smiling.

'Now what about it?' cried Ginger, and it must be confessed that in his tone there was more than a suspicion of satisfaction at this dramatic confirmation of his allegations.

'All you could talk of was an eye,' answered Biggles frostily. 'You said nothing about axes flying about.'

'I didn't wait for the axe,' replied Ginger emphatically. 'The eye was enough for me.'

Biggles took his automatic from his pocket and once more approached the companion-way. Gone was his earlier nonchalance. He might have been approaching a lion's den. 'Come out of that,' he shouted.

The answer was a peal of demoniac laughter that made the hairs on the back of Ginger's neck prickle. It did not come so much from the hatch as from the ice under their feet.

Biggles turned to the others. 'I know it sounds crazy, but there *is* somebody in the hulk,' he said soberly.

'Aye! It's a spook,' asserted the Skipper lugubriously. 'Come away, mon. Ye canna argue with a spook.'

'I have yet to see a spook that could argue with a soft-nosed forty-five-calibre bullet,' answered Biggles trenchantly.

But the Skipper, all his seafaring superstitions aroused, was as pale as Ginger. His Scotch accent broadened in his agitation. 'It's the de'il himsel',' he declared. 'I dinna like it. Let's awa'.'

'Away! Not on your life,' disputed Biggles grimly. 'I'm going to get to the bottom of this.' Again he called to the unseen occupant to show himself.

From the depths came a quavering moan. 'Go away. Go away. I found the gold. It's mine — mine.'

'I've got it,' cried the Skipper hoarsely. 'It's Manton — that's who it is. His puir numbed body lies outside in the cold ice, but his spirit canna rest.'

'Then it's time it could,' growled Biggles.

'The ship's haunted I tell ye,' cried the Skipper, backing away.

'Don't talk such rubbish,' rapped out Biggles. 'There's a man in this hulk. I don't know who he is and I don't know where he came from, but he's here, and, like Manton, he's gone out of his mind — either gold crazy or mad from loneliness. I'm going below to fetch him out.'

'He'll brain ye, mon. Drat the gold. Let's leave it?' implored the Skipper.

'I wasn't thinking so much about the gold,' answered Biggles slowly. 'I'm thinking about the man. We can't go away and leave the wretched fellow here.'

The Skipper was silent.

Said Ginger: 'It must have been *his* eye watching me.'

'No doubt of it,' replied Biggles. 'I apologise for doubting you, but you must admit that it took some believing.'

'And to think I was in the ship with — that!' Ginger shivered.

'Seems daft to get your head split open trying to save a man who doesn't want to be saved,' observed the Skipper gloomily. 'If ye go doon into yon hulk theer'll soon be two graves outside instead of one.'

Biggles nodded. 'Mebbe. It's an infernal nuisance. Who could have imagined such a situation?' He looked at Ginger: 'Remember what I told you about the unexpected always turning up on expeditions of this sort? Here you have a pretty example of it.'

'What are you going to do with the fellow if you do get

him out?' inquired Ginger.

'We'll talk about that when we've got him,' returned Biggles. Turning back to the opening he called: 'For the last time, are you coming out?'

'It's my gold you're after,' came the answer, screeched in the voice of a raving lunatic. 'I know who you are,' was the final surprising statement.

'Who am I?' called Biggles.

'Manton,' was the staggering reply. 'I saw your grave outside. I've heard you creeping about.'

Understanding dawned in Biggles' eyes. 'So that's it,' he said softly. 'The wretched fellow has gone crazy imagining Manton has returned from the grave to get the gold. Well, it's no use messing about any longer. I'm going in after him.'

'You must be madder than he is,' snorted the Skipper.

'We can't leave him here,' returned Biggles briefly; and with that he disappeared down the steps.

'We can't let him go down there alone,' cried Ginger in alarm, and ran forward to follow.

But the Skipper caught his arm and held him. 'You stay where you are,' he said shortly. 'I'll go.' Without waiting for the protest which he guessed would come, he, too, dived down the stairs.

Ginger took out his pistol and stood ready to move quickly should it be necessary. He noted that Biggles' prediction about the weather had come to pass. Fine snow was falling, reducing visibility to twenty or thirty yards. But before he had time to ponder the consequences this was likely to produce there came from somewhere below a wide yell and the crash of splintering ice. A moment later, from the place where he had seen the head, leapt the wild, unkempt figure of a man who sobbed and babbled in the manner of a terrified child. Ginger caught a glimpse of a white haggard face almost surrounded by a mane of tangled reddish hair. In his arms the man clutched an object which he recognised at once. It was one of the gold bars. Ginger moved quickly, thinking that the maniac — for maniac the man obviously was — intended to attack him. But this was not so. With a screech that was scarcely human the man jumped down to the level ice, fell, picked himself up, and still clutching the ingot, still sobbing, disappeared into the blur of falling snow. Ginger, not knowing what to do, in the end did nothing.

Biggles, followed by the Skipper, came scrambling out of the companion-way. 'Where is he? Which way did he go?' asked Biggles tersely.

Ginger pointed. 'That way. He's got a bar of gold with him.'

'Poor chap,' said Biggles sympathetically. 'A precious lot of good that'll do him out there. I'm afraid it's no use trying to follow him in these conditions. He probably knows his way about, and so may make his way back presently. That's what gold does to a man.'

'Who on earth can it be?' asked Ginger wonderingly.

'I know who he is,' put in the Skipper, surprisingly.

Biggles spun round. 'You know!' he exclaimed.

'Yes. It's Larsen, the Swede I told you about, who was lost when I was down here in the *Svelt*. Wandering about, he must have tumbled on the hulk by accident and has been living in it ever since. I only got a glimpse of him just now, but I remember that red hair. I should have known the voice. He was one of the few men I could trust. Mebbe that's why Lavinsky was content to leave him behind.'

'Well, that's settled the mystery of the sinister eye,

anyway,' said Biggles.

'What happened when you went below?' asked Ginger.

'Nothing much. The poor wretch was whining like a whipped dog. When he saw us coming he bolted. I went after him, but he crashed through some ice and disappeared. Apparently he knew of another way out.'

'Did you see the gold?'

'Yes. It's there — but it isn't all on the table any longer. Having seen you, Larsen must have guessed you'd come back, so he had started to hide the gold in a hole in the ice. Another half hour and he would have finished the job, in which case the metal would probably have remained in the ice for ever. We should never have found it. I should have assumed that Lavinsky had got here first and made off with the lot.'

'I'm surprised that Larsen didn't try to hide the stuff before to-day,' put in the Skipper.

'Why should he?' queried Biggles. 'About the last thing he'd expect was visitors. No doubt he was as surprised to see Ginger as Ginger was to see him — or rather, his eye. Had it been otherwise Ginger might have got his brains knocked out. As soon as Ginger bolted Larsen's first thought was to save his precious gold.'

The Skipper thrust his hands into his pockets. 'What are we going to do about him?'

'It's hard to know what to do, and that's a fact,' admitted Biggles. 'I don't think it's much use looking for the chap. If we go, I imagine he'll come back. If he does, the first thing he'll do will be to lug the gold out somewhere in the snow. It wouldn't be much use looking for it then. We can't let that happen. Our plan, therefore, must be to put the gold where he can't find it.'

'You mean — take it back to camp?' asked Ginger.

'Good gracious, no. That would be a tremendous task, taking far more time than we could afford.'

'But it will have to be carried to the machine sooner or later,' argued Ginger.

'Not at all. It would be a lot easier to bring the machine here.'

'True enough,' agreed Ginger. 'What about landing, though. Is there enough room?'

'I think so. I kept an eye open for possible landing areas as we walked here. It's quite flat between the hulk and the open water. What we'll do is carry the gold to a convenient place not far away, cover it with snow and then fetch the machine. If it comes to that, there's no need for everyone to walk back to camp. With Larsen on the loose, to be on the safe side someone should stay with the gold. You're looking tired, Ginger; perhaps you'll stay. The Skipper can come back with me to help clear up the camp. I don't think you've anything to fear from Larsen. If the snow continues he wouldn't be able to find you even if he tried. If it stops, he couldn't get to you without your seeing him. How does that sound?'

No one had a better plan so it was agreed.

'Are you going to start on the gold right away?' asked Ginger.

'We might as well,' answered Biggles. 'In fact, the sooner the better. The snow isn't as thick as it was. We may get a break but I'm afraid there's more snow to come. It's not so bad at the moment, at any rate.'

This was true. The snow had practically ceased, but the sky was still grey with a promise of more.

Ginger gazed across the desolate waste of the well-named White Continent. It was possible again to see a fair distance, but there was not a movement anywhere.

He wondered where the unfortunate Swede had managed to hide himself, and made a remark to that effect.

'He's probably busy hiding his lump of gold,' answered Biggles. 'There's nothing we can do about him for the time being. Let's get cracking on shifting the bullion.'

This proved to be a wearisome task, even though the gold had to be carried no great distance — merely to a point about one hundred yards from the open sea where, as the surface of the ice was smooth, and the snow thin, Biggles said he could put the aircraft down without much risk of accident. The ingots were heavy, but once hoisted on a shoulder one could be carried fairly easy. Transportation proceeded, therefore, at the rate of one bar per man per journey.

'I never thought the day would come when I should get tired of carrying gold,' remarked Ginger wearily, when, with the work finished, he sank down on the stack of precious metal.

'To move a ton of anything would be just as tiresome,' Biggles pointed out, perhaps unnecessarily. 'Still, it's finished now. I'll go with the Skipper back to camp, collect anything that we're likely to need, and bring the machine along. Sure you don't mind staying, Ginger?'

'No, I'll stay.'

'I shall be back in a couple of hours at the outside,' stated Biggles. 'As soon as the machine is in the air I'll get Grimy to make a signal to Algy asking him to fly down and help carry the stuff home. We'll light a smudge fire to show him where we are. He should have no difficulty in finding us.'

'What had I better do if Larsen comes for me?' asked

Ginger. 'I wouldn't like to use my gun on a lunatic.'

'A shot or two would probably scare him,' suggested Biggles. 'Personally, I don't think he'll worry you. He seemed terrified out of his wits by the mere sight of us, poor fellow. Our problem is how to get him home. However, we'll deal with that when the time comes. We'll get along now, while the weather's fair. See you presently.'

Biggles and the Skipper set off down the track the party had made on its outward journey.

Ginger watched them go. Quite content to rest for a while he arranged the gold bars in the manner of a seat and sat down to wait for the aircraft. The whimsical thought struck him that few people had been privileged to use a ton of pure gold as a seat. Actually, little of it could be seen, because the lower bars had sunk into the snow; and the thought occurred to him that if he should have to leave the spot for any reason he might have difficulty in finding it again. A short distance away stood one of the guide sticks he had used to mark his trail earlier in the day, so he fetched it, and arranged it in the heap like a miniature flag-staff. He could think of nothing else to do so he settled down, from time to time subjecting the landscape to a searching scrutiny for a possible sight of the castaway. But he saw nothing of him. The time passed slowly, and he began to understand ever more clearly why men marooned in this white world of silence soon went out of their minds. The loneliness became a tangible thing, an invisible enemy that stood ever at his elbow. The utter absence of sound weighed like lead upon his nerves.

It was with relief, therefore, that he heard in the far distance the sound of the Wellington's engines being started, for this at once seemed to put him in touch with the world of noise and bustle that he knew. Listening, he heard the drone rise to crescendo as the motors were run up. The sound died abruptly, and he could visualise Biggles sitting in the cockpit with the engines idling while he waited for the others to get aboard. Again came the vibrant roar and he imagined Biggles taking off. Good. In five minutes his vigil would end. But instead of this the note rose and fell several times in a manner which he could not understand. Then it died altogether. What had happened, he wondered. The only thing he could think of was, Biggles had for some reason taken off in the opposite direction and in so doing had run out of earshot. Presently he would hear him coming back. He waited, listening intently. The silence persisted. Not a sound of any sort reached his ears. What could have happened? At first he was merely disappointed, but as the minutes passed and still nothing happened his disappointment turned to uneasiness, and from uneasiness to apprehension.

Time passed. Still no sound came to break the frigid solitude. Over the world hung a trance-like calm, a calm that was the calmness of death. Sitting still, the intense cold began to strike at him with silent force. He looked at his watch, ticking inexorably its measurement of time. Biggles had been gone more than three hours. He knew then that he could not deceive himself any longer. Something had gone wrong. Biggles was in trouble. He stood up, staring in the direction of the camp. But he could see nothing. A few flakes of snow were now falling from the sky as grey as his mood.

CHAPTER 8

THE UNEXPECTED AGAIN

Ginger was right in his assumption that Biggles was in trouble; and it was trouble of a sort that Biggles thought he should have foreseen.

There had been no difficulty about the return journey to the camp. Everything was just as it had been left. Grimy sat by the fire with hot coffee waiting. Biggles and the Skipper each paused for a cup and then straight away set about the business of packing up, which consisted of no more than sorting out the most valuable equipment and sufficient food to see them over the next forty-eight hours. By that time, Biggles asserted, they should be back at the Falklands, and there was no point in loading the machine with unnecessary weight. The value of the cargo they were taking home would render negligible the cost of anything they left behind. The work, therefore, did not take long. The things required were securely stowed in the aircraft and the rest left where they were.

This done, Biggles climbed into the cockpit and ran up the engines. Satisfied and relieved to find that they were giving their revolutions he called to the others to get aboard and at once made ready to take off. The Skipper took the spare seat beside him, while Grimy went to his place at the wireless cabin with a message that Biggles had written for transmission to Algy, asking him to come straight out to help him to carry home the 'goods'.

When all was ready Biggles went through the usual formula for taking off. Nothing happened. The machine did not move. The engines bellowed. Still the aircraft did not move. He tried again, giving the engines as much throttle as he dare risk; but the machine remained as immobile as a rock. He throttled back and considered the situation; and it did not take him long to realise that only one thing could have happened. His landing chassis had either sunk in the snow or in some way had become attached to it. He switched off.

These, of course, were the sounds that Ginger had heard when he had supposed, naturally enough, that the machine had taken off, whereas in fact it had not left the ground.

Looking rather worried Biggles climbed down, and the others followed him. They found him on his knees examining the skis. He got up when the others joined him. 'I ought to be kicked for not thinking of it,' he remarked, with bitter self-denunciation.

'What's wrong, sir?' asked Grimy.

'The machine's been standing still long enough for the skis to become frozen to the snow. It must have been that slight rise in temperature that did it. I should have foreseen the possibility.'

'Won't the engines pull her off?' enquired the Skipper.

'This is an aircraft — not a tugboat,' returned Biggles. 'If I gave her full throttle and she came unstuck suddenly you'd see the unusual picture of an aeroplane turning a somersault. This is no place for exhibitions of that sort.'

'Can anything be done about it?'

'Yes, but it's going to take time, and Ginger is going to take a dim view of it if he's left sitting on his own. Still, he should take no harm. All we can do is cut the ice from under the skis and slide something under to prevent them from sticking again until we can get her off. Bring me the cold chisel, Grimy — the one we used for opening the packing cases.'

Grimy brought the tool.

'Now you can start knocking to pieces some cases to get some boards,' ordered Biggles. 'We'll stick them under as we go along.' Dropping on his knees he started chipping away the frozen snow. After a little while he paused to regard his work. 'We can do it,' he observed, 'but it's going to take a little while. What has happened is, the whole weight of the machine falling on the skis has pressed the snow till it's as hard as ice. At the same time they got stuck up. I seem to recall reading of a fellow who got into a similar jam. A few pieces of board would have prevented it. However, in this business there's always something new to learn.'

The work continued. The Skipper found a screwdriver and started on the second ski, while Grimy stood by and slipped boards under as the frozen snow was cleared away. The task was purely mechanical. The aircraft was in no danger. It was, as Biggles remarked, just one of those things. What caused him more anxiety than the machine was an occasional flurry of snow. It was evident that if the weather deteriorated further they were likely to be storm-bound, and Ginger might have some difficulty in getting back. His only shelter would be in the hulk, and if the Swede returned to it, as seemed likely, anything might happen. The thought spurred him to greater efforts.

As it turned out the job did not take as long as he expected, for as the work progressed the snow came away more easily. Moreover, by using a long board as a lever it became possible to prise the skis free. At any rate, by the end of an hour and a half, although the skis were not entirely clear, Biggles thought that the machine would move under the power of its engines. He climbed into the cockpit for a test, for, while it was not actually snowing, visibility was now so poor that he feared further delay might make flying impracticable. Starting the motors he eased the throttle open cautiously. For a moment the aircraft vibrated, shuddering: then a forward lurch told him what he wanted to know. The machine was clear.

'All right,' he shouted to the others. 'Get in. Bring some boards with you, Grimy. We must see this doesn't happen again.'

The undercarriage now did the work for which it had been designed. There was a certain amount of drag when the machine first moved forward, due, as Biggles expected, to ice particles still adhering to the skis; but as the aircraft gathered speed friction soon wiped them clean and the take-off became normal.

As soon as he was clear of the ice Biggles started to turn. Visibility, he discovered, was worse than it had appeared to be from ground level, and for that reason, knowing that there were no obstructions worth considering between him and his objective, he remained within sight of the 'carpet.' There was no horizon. All he could see was a small area of snow immediately below him. The position of the sun was revealed by a dull orange glow. Flying on even keel at five hundred feet he headed for the hulk, smiling faintly at the thought of what Ginger would have to say about his being left alone so long. A minute or two later, looking ahead along the ice-cliff he expected to see him; but when he failed to do so he was not particularly concerned because, as he now realised, the snow that had fallen would cover everything with a white mantle. Still, he thought it rather odd that Ginger did not stand up to give a wave. He half expected that he would have lit a fire to mark his position. However, Biggles could see the pile of ice that enclosed the hulk, so dismissing Ginger from his mind for a moment he concentrated on the anxious business of getting down. This, to his relief, he was able to accomplish without mishap. He hoped sincerely that it would be the last time he would have to do it. With the gold on board the next landing would be at the Falkland Islands.

As soon as the machine had run to a stop Grimy jumped down and thrust his boards under the skis to prevent a repetition of the trouble that had caused the delay. Biggles asked him if he had got the signal through to Algy. Grimy said that he had, but was unable to say anything more, owing to the short time at his disposal.

'You told him we'd found the wreck?' questioned Biggles.

'Yes, sir.'

'Good.' Biggles smiled. 'That should bring him along in a hurry. He ought to be here in a few hours. Meanwhile we can all have a rest while we're waiting. The trouble about all this daylight is, one tries to go on indefinitely without sleep. I only hope the weather doesn't get any worse. If it does, the other machine may have a job to find us.'

While he had been speaking Biggles had been looking around with a puzzled expression dawning on his face. 'Where the deuce is Ginger?'

Grimy looked around. The Skipper did the same. Neither answered.

A frown creased Biggles' forehead. 'I suppose we've come to the right place?'

'No mistake about that,' answered the Skipper. 'There's the hulk,' he pointed. 'We left Ginger over there.'

'That's what I thought,' said Biggles slowly. 'Well, he isn't there now. What the dickens can he have done with himself. That shower of snow was just enough to blot out the trail we made when handling the gold. Come to mention it I can't see the gold, either.'

'Could he have got cold and gone back into the hulk?' suggested the Skipper.

'He might have done, but with Larsen running wild I should say it's most unlikely,' muttered Biggles. He gazed round the landscape. 'What an extraordinary thing.'

'What beats me is why we can't see the gold,' put in Grimy.

'It would have snow on it,' reminded Biggles. 'Wherever Ginger may be, one thing is quite certain,' he went on. 'The gold will still be where we dumped it for the simple reason one man couldn't have moved it all in the time. Ginger wouldn't be likely to move it anyway, and he wouldn't allow Larsen to touch it. Still, it's very odd that we can't see it. I wonder if there's something deceptive about the visibility? It can play queer tricks in these conditions. Dash it all, the stuff *must* be here. Ginger must have dropped off to sleep and got a coating of snow over him. This is where we left him, over here.' Biggles began walking to the spot he had indicated, his pace increasing as he advanced. But still there was no sign of Ginger. Again he looked around. Then, speaking to the Skipper, he questioned: 'Are you certain this is the place?'

'Absolutely,' declared the Skipper without hesitation. 'What makes you doubt it?'

'I've got a feeling that something has changed.'

'What *could* change.'

Biggles shrugged his shoulders, unable to find a satisfactory answer to the question. In fact, the whole thing was a mystery for which he was quite unable to provide a solution. Again he stared at the frozen sterility about him, and then at the wreck, as if to convince himself that this was the place. Cupping his hands round his mouth he shouted, 'Ginger!'

There was no answer.

Biggles, looking completely nonplussed, stared at the Skipper. 'This beats anything and everything,' he muttered in a voice of bewilderment. 'This is the place where we left him — or else I'm going crazy.'

'Aye. This is the place all right,' assented the Skipper. 'We left him sitting on the stuff.'

'I know. And had he moved, or had Larsen come here, surely there would have been fresh tracks. What baffles me is there isn't a track anywhere.'

'I'd say he got browned off sitting here and went back to the ship where he could light a fire and maybe find something to eat,' opined Grimy.

Biggles shook his head. 'No. He didn't do that. You heard what he said. I'm sure nothing would have induced him to go near the hulk — at any rate, not while that madman is at large.'

The Skipper drew a deep breath. 'I give it up.'

Biggles showed signs of exasperation. 'The whole thing is absurd. He must be here. He wouldn't leave of his own accord, and ruling out Larsen, there's nobody here to make him move.' Biggles walked on a short distance towards the open water. 'He couldn't have gone that way, anyhow,' he declared.

'If he had he wouldn't have taken the gold with him,' observed the Skipper.

'That's what I mean,' returned Biggles helplessly. 'I've seen some queer things in my time but this beats them all.'

The Skipper let out a real seaman's hail.

There was no reply. The sound died away, leaving the sullen silence even more oppressive than before.

'If he was within half a mile he would have heard that,' asserted the sailor. He looked at Biggles. 'This reminds me of the Flying Dutchman,' he said nervously. 'You remember—'

Biggles broke in. 'Now don't start any more superstitious nonsense,' he requested curtly. 'There's nothing supernatural about this.' He strode away to the hulk. He did not stop when he reached it but went straight on down the companion-way. In a minute or two he was back. 'He isn't there,' he announced.

'There's nowhere else to look,' said the Skipper.

'If only the sky would clear I'd take the machine up and have a look round, but it's no use doing that in this infernal murk,' said Biggles irritably. Taking out his pistol he pointed the muzzle skywards and pulled the trigger. The report seemed dull and lifeless, but he listened for a reply. From far away out over the open sea came a faint report. He looked at the Skipper.

The Skipper shook his head. 'Echo,' he murmured. 'You get an echo from a big iceberg — or perhaps you could get one from that cloud just over our heads.'

Biggles looked dubious, but agreed that it was hardly likely that Ginger could have taken to the open sea, with the gold. Putting the pistol in his pocket he remarked: 'There must be an explanation of this. We've got to find it. That's all about it.'

CHAPTER 9

WHAT HAPPENED TO GINGER

The explanation of Ginger's uncanny disappearance was really perfectly simple. It may have been its very simplicity that caused it to be overlooked.

The statement that he had been left sitting on the gold was correct. He had not moved. There was no reason for him to move. He had no desire to see the inside of the hulk again so there was really nowhere for him to go even when he had become bored with sitting on his golden throne; and as the time passed he became very bored indeed. Not only was he bored, he was worried. He had, as he thought, heard the machine take off. It had not arrived. Obviously, something had gone wrong, and he nearly worried himself sick wondering what it could have been. But there was nothing he could do about it. Walking about would not help matters, so as he had no wish to collide with the deranged Swede he remained where he was, satisfied that Larsen would not be able to get to him without showing himself. His thoughts became sombre as he perceived all too clearly what his position would be if the aircraft never came. In that event, he pondered moodily, history looked like repeating itself. He would have to shoot Larsen or have his brains knocked out by an axe in the hands of a maniac. The prospect, he decided, was grim. He looked more often at the hulk, which he could just see in the bad light. Through the gloom, the pile of ice looked unpleasantly like a monstrous crouching apparition.

His fears took a more material turn when suddenly he experienced a queer sensation that the gold on which he was sitting had moved slightly. It was only the merest tremor yet he had been conscious of it. Or he thought he had. Was his imagination playing tricks? Why should he imagine such a thing? How could the gold move, anyway? Were his nerves in such a state? He stood up to rouse himself from the lethargy into which he had fallen, and tried to shake off the mood of depression which, he thought, must have been responsible for the illusion of movement. He promptly sat down again. He had not intended to. The movement was involuntary, induced, it seemed, by giddiness. Then he thought he understood. He was ill. Something was the matter with him — probably a recurrence of malaria contracted in the tropics. The idea took firm root when, a minute later, he experienced another quite definite wave of nausea, brought on by a feeling that the ground was rocking under him. Did they have earthquakes in the South Pole he wondered vaguely? Was that the answer? It seemed not impossible. Other countries had earthquakes, why not the Poles?

Cupping his chin in his hand he gazed across the desolation at the hulk. And as he looked at it his forehead puckered in a frown. Was it more imagination, or was the ice-encased ship farther away than it had been? Perhaps visibility had disimproved. That might produce such an effect. Then he noticed something else, something that brought him to his feet in haste. Between him and the hulk had appeared a black, irregular line, a line that widened as it appeared to cut a zig-zag course across the ice. He stood on the gold for a better view, and then he understood. A portion of the main pack ice had broken away, and he was on the piece that had come adrift.

Wondering why he had not realised at once what was happening he ran towards the line of water that now separated him from the mainland. His one concern was his personal safety. By the time he had reached the water he saw to his consternation that it was already some eight or ten feet wide, which was too wide for a jump from such a slippery take off. Swiftly his eyes ran along the gap. They stopped when they came to a place where it was still only two or three feet across. He raced towards it. But the ice was moving too, and by the time he had reached the spot the gap was again too wide. He ran on, still looking for a place where he might get across, hoping even to find a spot where the floe had not actually parted from the parent ice. There was no such place. In sheer panic now he tore along the edge of his floating island; but it was no use. Everywhere the gap was too wide, and every passing second saw it wider. Bitterly he regretted that he had not risked a jump while there was still a chance. Breathing heavily he stared at the black water, six feet below him. There could be no question of swimming. The cold would be paralyzing. In any case, it would be impossible to climb up the sheer face of ice. So there he stood, his thoughts in a turmoil, watching the gap yawn ever wider with slow, relentless force. The hulk, his only landmark, became an indistinct object in a white shadowless world. Presently that too disappeared.

He knew there could be no other way of escape, but in sheer desperation he looked for one. All around were floes, rafts of ice like the one he was on. All appeared to be motionless, but he knew they must be moving. Some were quite close, but all were detached, so there was no point in leaving his own. In the end he had to face the fact that there was nothing he could do. Indeed, as far as he could see there was nothing anyone could do, for while the floe he was on was not small, it was not big enough for the aircraft to land on even if Biggles should discover his predicament. He had, he thought, one chance, provided Biggles came quickly; for the gap between him and the mainland told him that the floe was moving ever faster, presumably as it felt the affect of a current. The aircraft, in view of its long over-water journey, carried as part of its equipment a collapsible rubber dinghy. It would take a little time to inflate and launch, and the employment of it in the floating ice-fields would be risky, for not only might it be crushed between two pieces of ice but one small piece of the razor-edged stuff would certainly puncture it. But before it could be used Biggles would have to find him; and there was good reason to suppose that Biggles himself was in serious difficulties or he would have been back long ago.

The floe was now some distance from the stable pack-ice, and he had an idea that his drift was towards the north-east. Visualising the map he perceived that if the floe maintained that direction it would eventually bring up against the long, north-pointing arm of the Graham Peninsula, the best part of a hundred miles away. What would happen then was a matter for speculation. It would not affect him, anyhow, because long before the ice had travelled that distance he would have died from hunger and exposure. Should the floe find itself in the grip of a more northerly current — as obviously some did, for he had seen them on the way down — then the ice would eventually melt, dropping him and the gold into the deepest sea. The gold! He laughed bitterly. He could now understand why Last, when he had made his desperate bid for life in a small boat, hadn't bothered about the gold. At that moment Ginger would have swopped all his gold bars for a dinghy, no matter how dilapidated as long as it would float for twenty minutes.

Standing on the edge of the ice, as near as he could get to the main pack, he watched it gradually fade into the background. He knew it was no use shouting, for Biggles was not there to hear him. It was ironic that the only man who might be within hail was a raving lunatic. After a while, realising that he could do no good by standing there, he walked slowly back to the gold and sat down to think the matter over. Not that there was much to think about.

So this, he pondered miserably, was the end of their adventure — at any rate, the end of his. How many mariners, he wondered, had found themselves in the same melancholy plight, since men had begun their search for the great Southern Continent hundreds of years before his time. A good many, no doubt. And there would be more. Something of the sort had happened to Larsen. He had managed to get ashore, and a lot of good it had done him. Ginger could only hope that his fate would not be so long drawn out. A ghastly picture of himself and Larsen fighting it out in the hulk for possession of the gold, as Last and Manton had done, floated into his mind. He dismissed it with a shiver, perceiving that such thoughts were a certain way to madness.

Biggles, he feared, would never come now. Something had happened to him. He could not imagine what it was. The engines, which he had heard, seemed to be in order. Was he, too, marooned somewhere in this dismal world of everlasting ice? How he hated the stuff.

All around him he could hear it growling and crunching as the floes ground into each other. Once he watched it happen, quite close to where he sat. He saw the ice splinter as the two pieces drove against each other; watched them locked in frozen embrace drift away into the murk. From an inside pocket he produced a bar of chocolate. He ate it slowly and deliberately, and was surprised to find that he could do so without emotion, although it was probably the last thing he would ever eat. He was almost glad that he had no provisions with him, for they would only prolong the inevitable end.

He did not take account of the passing of time, but it must have been about an hour later that he heard a sound that brought him to his feet with a rush. It was the drone of an aircraft. It sounded a long way off, but in his desperate case it brought a new hope, for it did at least tell him that Biggles was still alive. Listening he heard the aircraft take off, which meant that the machine was, after all, still airworthy. He could not see it, of course; it was too far off for that; but he could more or less follow its course. He judged it was on its way to the hulk. He waited for it to land, but when it did he was appalled by its distance away. It seemed impossible that he could have drifted so far in so short a time. Or was the sound deceptive, muffled, perhaps, by the low cloud? He could not even hazard a guess as to the actual distance in terms of measurement. It might be a mile, he thought; it might be two or even three. Taking out his pistol he fired a shot into the air and listened for an answering shot. None came. He knew the sound would be very faint, too faint to be heard if Biggles or the others happened to be talking, or making a noise of any sort.

He sat down again, staring in the only direction from

which deliverance could come. Biggles by this time would be looking for him, wondering what had become of him. He tried shouting, but in the vastness the sound seemed a mere bleat, flat and futile. Even the skuas, with their high pitched note, could make more noise than that, he reflected bitterly. He sprang to his feet again as from the far distance came a faint pop. Could it have been a shot? Taking his pistol again he fired it in the direction from which the sound had come and then listened breathlessly for a reply. It did not come. He could have thrown his weapon into the sea from very impotence. No wonder Larsen had gone out of his mind in such a place where even a pistol seemed unable to make its usual healthy explosion.

A feeling of utter futility grew on him. It seemed to be getting colder, too, and in order to keep his circulation going he had to stamp about and buff his arms. His breath hung in the air like smoke. If only the weather would clear, he thought petulantly, as he paced up and down, stamping his feet. Even the weather was against him, although he did not lose sight of the fact that it might easily be worse. But in clear weather Biggles might still be able to see him from the shore. From the air, when Biggles took off to look for him, as he would, he would be spotted at once. Algy would soon be coming too. There was a chance that he might see him — but not in this dismal gloom.

Time wore on. Ginger was deadly tired but he dare not rest. Apart from being buried under snow should there be another storm, or becoming frozen in his sleep, he might miss something, perhaps an attempt at rescue. All the same, with the visibility factor so low he did not think Biggles would risk flying low over the open sea for fear of colliding with one of the big bergs which, even on a clear day, were not always easy to see. To fly high would be useless.

For a long time, it seemed, Ginger paced up and down the ice, sometimes resting on the heap of gold, staring into space, striving to probe with his eyes the intangible barrier that surrounded him on all sides. And while he sat thus, brooding on the little things which make all the difference between life and death, the deceitful atmosphere played on him another trick. He saw a ship. He closed his eyes for a moment and looked again. It was still there. He could see it distinctly. A minute earlier it had not been there, he was sure of that. Now it was as large as life, as the saying goes, clear in every detail. What sort of phenomenon was this, he wondered? Could there be such a thing as a mirage in polar waters, such as he had seen in the deserts of Arabia? Or was this the beginning of madness?

For a little while yet he sat still, unable to believe his eyes — or if the truth must be told, not daring to believe them. But when he saw men moving on the deck and the throb of an engine reached his ears he knew that a miracle had happened. A ship *was* there. A real ship. Springing to his feet he let out a wild yell.

That it had been heard he knew at once from the way the men stopped what they were doing to stare at him. Their amazement, he thought, as the vessel turned slowly towards him, would be no less than his.

It may seem odd that the possible identity of the craft did not occur to him; but it must be remembered that, situated as he was, with a miserable fate confronting him, the gold and everything to do with it had for all practical purposes ceased to exist. He assumed, naturally, that the ship was one of those whalers or sealers which on rare occasions penetrated to the southern extremity of the open water in search of prey. Apart from that, his one overwhelming emotion was thankfulness that by a chance little short of miraculous he was saved. He could have shouted from sheer relief. Instead, he held himself in hand, and stood calmly awaiting deliverance.

But when his eyes wandered idly to the bows of the ship and he read the name *Svelt* his exuberance died abruptly. Even then it took him a moment or two to recall the association of the word and realise its full significance. *Svelt.* Lavinsky's ship. So that was it. Of course. What a fool he had been not to guess it at once. Not that it would have made much difference. He would still have welcomed it. He would have welcomed any craft. Anything was better than dying slowly on a floating island of ice.

Then he remembered the gold. What should he do about it? He had to think quickly because the *Svelt* was now swinging round to come alongside the ice, and a man was already standing ready to throw him a line. His brain worked swiftly. Lavinsky must not suspect the incredible truth — that the little hump of snow behind him covered the thing he had come to fetch.

Knowing something of Lavinsky's character, Ginger saw clearly that if the man realised the gold was there his respite would be shortlived. There would be no question of sharing it, or anything like that. Lavinsky would take the gold and probably knock him on the head as the easiest way of disposing of an undesirable witness. This done he would simply turn round and sail home in triumph, while Biggles would for ever after be in ignorance of what had happened. The thing, obviously, was to say nothing. The gold would have to take its chance. It was not for him to jeopardise his life by mentioning it. Lavinsky, no doubt, would go on to the ice-pack and proceed with his search. There, sooner or later, he would run into Biggles. He, Ginger, would then tell Biggles what had happened, and leave him to deal with the newcomers. Glancing over his shoulder he saw that the gold was pretty well covered with snow. Under the pretext of stretching his legs as if to relieve stiffness he kicked a little more snow over the one or two places where it had been brushed off by his garments. One thing was quite certain, he thought whimsically. However well endowed with imagination Lavinsky might be, he would hardly expect to find the gold where it actually was — floating on the high seas on a slab of ice.

The ship felt its way alongside. A rope came swishing across the ice. Grabbing it, Ginger allowed himself to be hauled up to the deck, where he found himself facing a semi-circle of spectators. The men, a hard-looking lot, appeared all the tougher from the heavy garments they wore against the cold. Most wore balaclava helmets. Some were obviously Asiatics.

The first question put was the obvious one. A man in a greasy blue jacket and peaked cap stood a little in front of the others. Ginger guessed it was Lavinsky. He was not a big man. His face was pale, thin, and carried prominent cheek-bones that suggested Slav ancestry. His eyes, set close together, were cold and grey, and held a calculating quality which provided a good indication of his character. He looked at Ginger as though he might have been a freak, although in the circumstances this was understandable.

'Where have you come from?' he asked in English which, while good, held a curious accent.

'From the pack-ice,' replied Ginger, noting with satisfaction that the ship was now edging away from the floe.

'What were you doing there?'

'Exploring.'

'What's the name of your ship?'

'I haven't got a ship,' answered Ginger. 'I'm a member of a British air exploration party. I was sitting near the edge of the ice, resting while the others were away, when the part I was on broke off and went adrift. By the time I'd realised it I was too far out to get back. There was nothing I could do about it. The plane was away on a flight. I heard it come back but I couldn't make the crew hear me. I'd just about given up hope when you appeared.'

'Huh! I reckon you were kinda lucky,' observed the man cynically.

Ginger agreed. But the man's next question shook him.

'I reckon,' said he slowly, 'you're a member of the party that found the ship.'

Ginger's astonishment was geniune. 'Ship,' he echoed. 'What ship?'

'We've got radio,' was the sneering answer. 'A little while ago we picked up a message from someone saying the ship had been found.'

Then, of course, Ginger understood what had happened. Biggles had sent a signal to Algy and the *Svelt* had intercepted it. There could hardly be two exploring parties on the polar ice so Lavinsky knew who he was. In any case there seemed to be no reason why he should not stick to the truth. 'Yes,' he agreed. 'There is an old hulk fast in the ice near our camp. If you happen to land there you'd better keep clear of it though.'

The man's manner changed. 'Why?'

'Because there's a madman in it,' answered Ginger casually. 'By the way, whom am I talking to?'

'My name's Lavinsky and I'm the master of this ship. What's this about a madman?'

'When we went up to have a look at the wreck, not expecting to find anybody on board, we had a shock when somebody slung an axe at us. Then he started howling. I got a glimpse of him — a biggish fellow with red hair.'

Lavinsky spun round to face his crew. 'Red hair. You heard that? I reckon we know who *he* is, boys. So that's where he went. Well, I guess we can deal with him.' Speaking again to Ginger, Lavinsky went on: 'Did you get into the ship?'

Ginger smiled ruefully. 'I was in it for about three minutes. Then I caught sight of an eye watching me through the ice so I went out again in a hurry.'

Lavinsky hesitated, and Ginger knew why. The question of paramount importance was now to come, but Lavinsky was loath to show his hand. In the end he had to — more or less.

'Was there anything — er — valuable, in this old hulk?' he enquired.

It was a tense moment. Ginger could almost feel the entire crew hanging on his answer. 'What do you mean by valuable?' he parried.

'Gold, for instance.' Lavinsky spoke as if he could not bear to wait a moment longer.

'I shouldn't think there's any gold in that ship,' answered Ginger, smiling faintly. 'I'm pretty sure there isn't,' he went on. 'If there is, as far as I'm concerned you can have it all.' In the circumstances, considering the character of his interrogator, he felt that such dissemblement was justified.

'We'll go and see,' said Lavinsky. 'You'd better get below.'

'Thanks,' acknowledged Ginger, feeling that however dangerous his position might be now, his prospects of survival were brighter than they had been half an hour earlier.

CHAPTER 10

A SHOCK FOR BIGGLES

Meanwhile, while Ginger was having his lonely adventure on the high seas, Biggles was standing by the aircraft, completely at a loss for once to know what to do. It was another piece of ice, quite a small piece, breaking away from the main ice-field, that in the end provided the solution to the mystery of Ginger's disappearance. He realised then what must have happened and he was angry with himself for not thinking of it at once. Like all problems, when the answer became available it seemed so simple.

His first inclination was to get back into the machine and make a search of the open water; and no doubt in his anxiety he would have done so, had not the Skipper pointed out two factors that counselled prudence. In the first place there was no clear indication of the size of the piece of ice that had broken away, carrying Ginger with it, for in the business of transporting the gold no one had paid much attention to the water line at that point. Had it been only a small piece, the Skipper asserted, the weight of the gold, if it happened to be on one side, might have been sufficient to overturn it. Even if the floe did not overturn, said the Skipper, it might have taken on a list at such an angle as to cause Ginger and the gold to slide off. Secondly, visibility was bad, and showed little sign of improving. With big bergs about, low flying, as would be necessary if the flight was to serve any useful purpose, would be little less of suicidal. Why not wait a little while to give visibility a chance to improve, suggested the Skipper. The clouds overhead might pass. If Ginger was in fact adrift on a piece of ice another hour would make little difference to the actual situation. A mile or two, one way or the other, could not vitally affect the issue.

This was sound reasoning and Biggles was the first to admit it. What he realised, too, even better than the Skipper, was this; once he lost sight of his position, in such a poor light it might not be easy to find again. The landing too would be an added risk, not to be ignored. It was not as if only his own life was at stake. There was the Skipper and Grimy to be considered. Whether he took them with him in the machine, or left them on the ice, he would be subjecting them to risks which were manifestly unfair — at any rate, unless there was absolutely no alternative. As the Skipper put it there was an alternative. He would wait a little while to see if the weather improved.

Lighting a cigarette while he thought the matter over, new difficulties presented themselves. Suppose he did find Ginger, what could he do about it? The floe would have to be a very big one for him to land on it. If he couldn't land, how was he to pick him up? If he located him, the only way of getting to him would be by means of the rubber dinghy. He then considered launching the dinghy anyway, and again it was the Skipper who pointed out the inadvisability of such a course. To paddle about haphazard amongst the ice-floes would, he alleged, be sheer madness. It would only need two small pieces of ice to close in on such a frail craft and the dinghy would be lost, and their lives with it. It would be better, he argued, to save it until they could see what they were doing.

Again Biggles was forced to agree that this argument made sense, yet it went against the grain to just stand there doing nothing.

Ginger was not Biggles' only worry. By this time Algy and Bertie would be on their way. They would expect him to be on hand, not only to reveal his position but to indicate a safe place for them to land. This in itself, in the present weather conditions, would be a serious operation. Obviously, brooded Biggles, he couldn't be in two places at once. If he went out to look for Ginger, and was still out when the reserve machine arrived, the lives of Algy and Bertie would be jeopardised. Yet by staying where he was he felt he was abandoning Ginger. However, in the end he did nothing. Leaning against the machine he smoked cigarette after cigarette to steady his nervous impatience, all the time watching the sky for the first sign of an improvement. Out on the open water ice-floes growled and splintered. Sometimes a piece of ice would drift past. He watched a floe go by.

'The experts are right,' he remarked presently. 'The general drift is a bit north of east. That means that this stuff is drifting past our old camp, and if the direction is maintained the ice may pile up against the Graham Peninsula.'

'That's about it,' confirmed the Skipper. 'If the ice drifts that way so does everything else. I've often seen bergs carrying rocks and stones which the ice must have torn from the land in shoal water. It must all end up in the same place.'

'We'll remember that when we start searching,' said Biggles. He looked up. 'Is it my fancy or is the cloud lifting a bit?'

'Aye, she's lifting,' agreed the Skipper. He glanced around. 'I can't help wondering what Larsen has done with himself. Funny where he went to.'

'He's probably watching us from a distance,' replied Biggles. 'There's nobody more cunning that a fellow out of his mind. The gold is his particular mania, of course. When he discovers that it's gone he's liable to do anything, so we'd better keep our eyes open. I think we might have a snack and a cup of tea. By the time we've finished, if the weather continues to improve it should be good enough for a reconnaisance. Anyway, whatever it's doing I'm going to look for Ginger. We can't leave him out there. Get the kettle boiling, Grimy.'

Half an hour later the weather was no longer in doubt. It had improved considerably. The sky was clearing, due possibly to a fall in the thermometer.

'I'll tell you one thing,' observed the Skipper. 'There's going to be a cracking frost to-night.'

'It can do what it likes as long as it stays clear,' answered Biggles, who, now that he could do something, was feeling better. 'Grimy, you'll stay here and get a good smudge fire going,' he ordered, as he moved towards the aircraft. Having reached it, he paused for a last look round, for it was now possible to see for some distance. Looking out to sea, to his unbounded amazement he saw a ship creeping through the floating ice towards the main shelf. It was in a very curious voice that he said: 'Skipper, come here. Can you see what I see?'

The Skipper, who had been on the far side of the machine, joined him. 'Aye,' he said slowly. 'I can see more than you can. I know that ship. I ought to, considering the time I've put in on her bridge. It's the *Svelt*. Looks as if Lavinsky's arrived.'

'That's what I thought,' returned Biggles evenly. 'This alters things — alters them considerably.'

'What are you going to do about it?' enquired the Skipper, a hint of urgency about his tone.

'Do? Nothing.'

'They're a tough lot.'

'I've met tough people before.'

'Well, I reckon we ought to do something,' asserted the Skipper. 'If you suppose we can all settle down nice and friendly on the same piece of ice you've got another think coming. It would be easier to settle down with a pack of wolves. Lavinsky's bad — real bad.'

'What do you suggest we do — run away?'

'Well no, not exactly.'

'I should think not,' returned Biggles frostily. 'We'll wait here and see what they have to say. They're heading this way because they must have seen the machine. They haven't done anything to us yet, so we'll give them the benefit of the doubt. If Lavinsky starts making a nuisance of himself he'll find I can be awkward, too.'

'But you can't take on that bunch,' declared the Skipper. 'If Lavinsky's got the same crew, and I reckon he has, there'll be a score of 'em.'

'Numbers aren't everything,' returned Biggles quietly. 'I've met that sort before. They're never as smart as they think they are. And anyway, Lavinsky has as much right to be here as we have, so long as he behaves himself. If we tried to stop him landing, and he made a complaint, we might find ourselves legally in the wrong. If there's going to be a rough house we'll let him start it. I'm by no means sure he will though. His only concern is the gold, so he'll probably be all right until he discovers it's gone. My main concern is Ginger. I may ask Lavinsky to turn his ship round to look for him. The *Svelt* would be a much better vehicle for the job than an aircraft.'

'I still reckon he's got a nerve, coming in here like this,' said the Skipper.

'In what way?'

'With all this loose ice about. The sea's full of it. He found a way in but that ain't to say he'll find a way out. If he happens to find himself between two big floes he's likely to finish up like the hulk behind us.'

'Men will take any risks when there's gold in the offing,' observed Biggles.

'All the same, he must be daft to take such a chance while ice is breaking off all along the shelf. I've been watching it.'

'Some people might say we're not entirely sane ourselves, bringing an aircraft to a place like this,' Biggles pointed out.

'Aye, mebbe you're right at that,' concurred the Skipper with a sigh.

The *Svelt* came on, feeling her way cautiously. That the aircraft had been seen was obvious from the way the crew had collected forward to look. Biggles returned the inspection. Indeed, he went so far as to raise a hand in greeting.

The ship came right in, for the water was deep right up to the edge of the shelf. Fenders were thrown out and the vessel edged alongside.

'That's Lavinsky, the fellow in the peaked cap,' the Skipper told Biggles quietly. 'The other two I told you about, the two I called Shim and Sham, are on each side of him. They don't say much, but they don't miss much, either. I reckon they're the partners who finance Lavinsky.'

'Lavinsky was smart enough to get the position of the hulk when you were here with him the last time,' murmured Biggles.

'He couldn't have come straight here,' argued the Skipper. 'If he had we should have passed him on the way down. I'd say he took too much westerly, and finding he was wrong, worked his way along the shelf looking for the wreck.'

Biggles did not answer. He was staring at another figure that had appeared on deck. He caught the Skipper by the arm. 'By thunder! They've got him,' he ejaculated.

'Got who?'

'Ginger. There he is, on deck. They must have picked him up. That's a load off my mind, anyway. That probably explains it.'

'Explains what?'

'Why the *Svelt* came in here. Ginger would have to tell them we were here to account for being here himself. There was no reason why he shouldn't if it comes to that. I wonder what else he told them.'

'If he's told them that we got the gold it won't be long before bullets start flying,' declared the Skipper grimly.

'He hasn't told them anything of the sort.'

'Mebbe they've got the gold. We left Ginger sitting on it.'

'That doesn't mean he was still sitting on it when they picked him up,' disputed Biggles. 'We don't know about that; but what I do know is, Lavinsky hasn't got the gold under his hatches.'

'How do you work that out?'

'Because if he had he'd have turned his ship north, not south. There would have been no need for him to hazard his ship coming here if he'd already got what he came for — unless, of course, he was decent enough to give Ginger a lift back.'

The Skipper laughed shortly. 'Ha! I can't see Lavinsky doing that.'

'Keep that muffler up over your face,' said Biggles softly. 'I don't think he's realised yet who you are.'

Further conversation of an intimate nature was prevented by the arrival on the ice of Lavinsky and his owners, Shim and Sham. Lavinsky spoke first. 'I've brought one of your boys along,' he announced.

'So I see,' replied Biggles civilly. 'Much obliged to you. I was worried about him.'

'He tells me you're down here on an exploring trip for the British Government.'

Biggles smiled faintly. 'That's right. This is a Government outfit.'

At this point, now that he was close, Lavinsky appeared to notice the Skipper for the first time. That recognition was instantaneous was obvious from the way his expression changed. So had his voice changed, when he said: 'So *you're* here.'

'Looks like it,' answered the Skipper.

Lavinsky nodded. 'Now I get it.' He hesitated as if uncertain how to proceed. Then he went on: 'Well, I reckon it's no use beating about the bush,' he said slowly. 'Where's the wreck?'

The Skipper pointed. 'She's suffered a fair bit of damage since you were here last. Her masts are down and she's well under the ice.'

Lavinsky regarded the ice that hid the actual timbers of the vessel. 'I see,' he murmured. 'Is the gold still in her?'

'No.'

Lavinsky's eyes narrowed as they rested on the Skipper. 'How do I know that?'

'Go and look for yourself.'

'Where is it?'

Biggles stepped into the conversation. 'That's just what we should like to know.'

'You mean — you haven't got it?'

'Should we be here if we had?'

'Are you kidding?' Lavinsky's eyes grew dark with suspicion.

Biggles raised a shoulder. 'There's the hulk, there's my machine. You won't find any gold in either. You have my permission to look.'

'Permission!' Lavinsky's tone hardened. 'Who do you think you are to give me permission to do anything? I do what I like.'

'I wouldn't start talking like that,' suggested Biggles quietly. 'I'd better warn you that the salvage of that ship has been acquired by the British Government. I'm here under Government orders, with Government equipment, to collect anything worth taking home. Which means, Mr Lavinsky, that before you can enter that hulk you have to ask my permission, I being the head of the salvage operation.'

Lavinsky turned an evil eye on Ginger, who had now come ashore and was standing beside Biggles. His whole attitude was one of calculating malice. 'This is a different tale from the one you told me,' he said harshly.

'Not at all,' denied Ginger. 'I answered your questions fairly. If I didn't volunteer any details it was because I saw no reason to. It wasn't my place to, anyway.'

Lavinsky considered the matter. He looked at his two companions, but their faces were expressionless and he found no inspiration there. He took a cigar from an inside pocket, put it in his mouth, lit it, and flung the match down. 'Well, what are we going to do?' he demanded viciously.

'Do about what?' asked Biggles.

'The gold? What else do you think I'm interested in?'

'If you're asking for my advice, here it is,' returned Biggles smoothly. 'As there's nothing for you to do here you'd better turn round and make for home before you get gripped in the ice and finish up like that hulk.'

'Me go home? With nothing? Not likely.'

'Please yourself. I can't stand here talking any longer. I've got things to do.'

'How about splitting the gold two ways,' suggested Lavsinky. 'I reckon you could do with some of it, and I ain't greedy.'

'At the moment there's no gold to split, even if I agreed to your proposal. Which I wouldn't because as I have already told you, it belongs to the people for whom I happen to be working,' answered Biggles coldly.

'You say it isn't in the hulk?'

'It is not.'

'Then Larsen must have hid it somewhere. This boy of yours told me he was living in the hulk.'

'He was,' confirmed Biggles. 'I don't know where he is now. He greeted me with an axe and then bolted. He's mad, so be careful if you run into him.'

Lavinsky laughed unpleasantly. 'You needn't worry about me,' he said meaningly.

'I'm not worrying about you,' answered Biggles calmly. 'I'm just warning you, that's all. I say the man is insane, and as you know it you've no excuse for anything that may happen. To make my meaning quite clear. I'm not prepared to stand here and see murder done, if that's what's in your mind. Larsen was once a member of your crew. You abandoned him — oh yes, I heard about that — so you're responsible for what's happened to him. In those circumstances the least you can do is treat him decently and take him to a place where he can get medical attention. With a ship you are better able to do that than I am with an aircraft.'

Lavinsky drew deeply at his cigar and expelled the smoke slowly. 'I'll decide what to do with him when I've found him,' he stated. A sneer crept into his voice as he went on. 'Meanwhile, have I your permission to look through the hulk?'

'You have. That, of course, doesn't give you the right to take anything away.'

Lavinsky looked sideways at his companions and jerked his head towards the wreck. 'Come on,' he said. Followed by his companions he strode away to the hulk, went up the ice steps and disappeared down the companion-way.

Biggles watched them go. 'Things seem to be getting complicated,' he murmured. Then, turning to Ginger, he inquired: 'Well, what have you to say for yourself?

It did not take Ginger long to narrate the unpleasant adventure that had befallen him and the remarkable manner of his escape.

'So you left the gold on the ice,' said Biggles thoughtfully, when he had finished.

'What else could I do?'

'Nothing,' admitted Biggles. 'Had you told Lavinsky that the gold was under his nose you wouldn't be here now — neither would the *Svelt*. Have you any idea of which way you were drifting when you were picked up?'

'Slightly north of east, as near as I could tell.'

'How big was the floe you were on?'

'Fairly big — say, about three acres altogether.'

'What shape was it?'

'Wide at one end and narrow at the other. Something

like the shape of a pear, only the narrow end tailed off to a point.'

'Not big enough to land on?'

'No.'

'Would you know it if you saw it again?'

'I think so — provided, of course, there weren't a lot more like it. I should know for certain if I could get close because I fixed one of my sticks in the gold. I doubt if you'd see it from a distance, but it does at least mark the position of the gold on the floe. Luckily the gold was under snow; that's why Lavinsky didn't see it.'

At this juncture Lavinsky and his companions reappeared and rejoined the party standing by the aircraft. 'I reckon you're right,' conceded Lavinsky, speaking to Biggles. 'Somebody's been in since I was last there — left food and stuff lying about. The gold's gone.'

'You're telling me what I've already told you,' replied Biggles.

'Sure. But I wanted to —' Lavinsky's eyes went to the aircraft.

'You still think it might be in my machine?' suggested Biggles softly.

'It could be.'

'I told you it is not.'

'All the same, it might be.'

'If I say it isn't, it isn't,' said Biggles shortly. 'Still, you can go and look if you like. I only wish the stuff was on board because I could then turn my tail to this perishing country.'

'Yes, I suppose that's right,' said Lavinsky in a low voice, as if speaking to himself. Nevertheless, he walked over to the machine and looked in the cabin.

When he came back Biggles said: 'Well, I hope

you're satisfied.'

Lavinsky did not answer. To his companions he muttered: 'Let's get aboard and talk it over.' They went back to the *Svelt*.

'We'd better talk things over, too,' suggested Biggles. 'I think the aircraft is the best place.' He led the way to the cabin.

CHAPTER 11

MOVE AND COUNTER-MOVE

When they were all assembled in the cabin Biggles opened the debate by saying: 'Well, this is a pretty state of affairs. Queer, isn't it, how shows of this sort never seem to run smoothly. That piece of ice on which we piled the gold must have been there for years, but it had to choose to-day, of all days, to break off. Yesterday it wouldn't have mattered. To-morrow it wouldn't have mattered, either. But no. It had to be to-day, at the very hour Ginger decided to sit on it. That's how things go. To complicate matters, Lavinsky rolls up. In a way that may have been lucky; no doubt Ginger thought so at the time, although I still think we had a good chance of finding him without any help from Lavinsky. But that's past history. The question is, what next?'

'How about looking for the gold,' suggested Ginger.

'I have every intention of looking for it,' replied Biggles. 'But how are we going to set about it without Lavinsky realising what we're doing. He's sick at losing the gold and he won't give up easily. He's boiling up for trouble even now. If it comes to war someone will get hurt, that's certain — although as long as it isn't Lavinsky he won't care. He's the type that soon gets my goat, and I'm standing for no nonsense from him. But even with Algy and Bertie here the odds would still be on his side, so if we can get the gold and clear out without a stand-up fight, so much the better. There's nothing we can do for the moment, because we've got to wait for Algy to come in. He should be here in half an hour or so. When we hear him coming we'll light a smudge fire and mark out a landing ground. As soon as he gets safely down we'll explain the position to him and then start looking for this pear-shaped floe of Ginger's. I'm afraid locating it is going to be no easy job; and even if we do locate it, to get the gold into the aircraft without Lavinsky spotting what's going on will be another pretty problem. There is this about it; we shall soon know the worst, for the simple reason we haven't enough petrol to cruise about indefinitely.'

'What do you reckon Lavinsky will do, now he's satisfied that we haven't got the gold and it isn't in the hulk?' asked Ginger.

'I wouldn't say he's satisfied,' returned Biggles. 'He must know the gold can't be far away, so as soon as he gets over the shock of finding us here he'll start looking for it, or try to work out what could have become of it. He won't leave here while there's the slightest chance of it still being in the vicinity, you can bet your boots on that. Like us, he's chewing it over from his angle. I don't think he'll guess that we've found the gold and moved it, because, on the face of it, there was no earthly reason why we should do anything of the sort. All he knows is, the gold isn't where it was when he last saw it. The stuff couldn't have moved itself so somebody must have shifted it. Only one person has been here as far as he knows, and he was here long enough to distribute the stuff all over the landscape if he felt like it — Larsen. The first thing he'll do, then, is look for the Swede. Were I in his position I should probably do the same thing, although I should ask myself why should Larsen move the gold knowing perfectly well that the chances of anyone landing here were remote.'

'Larsen's mad, and who can say what a madman will do,' murmured the Skipper.

'True enough,' agreed Biggles. 'Anyhow, the stuff has gone, and ruling out the possibility of anyone else coming here, only Larsen could have moved it. Of course, Lavinsky won't overlook the possibility of it being hidden somewhere in the hulk, so it's quite likely that he'll pull the timbers apart looking for it. There's nowhere else for him to look. It wouldn't be much use starting to search the whole landscape. I only hope it doesn't occur to him to wonder why *we* didn't pull the ship to pieces in a hunt for it, because if he starts thinking on those lines he may tumble on the truth — that we know more about the gold than we pretend. It boils down to this. I think Lavinsky will thoroughly search the ship. When that fails he'll look for Larsen, hoping that if he can find him he'll be able to tell them where the gold is hidden.'

'Larsen wouldn't tell Lavinsky anything,' put in the Skipper. 'He knows what sort of a man he is. Mad though he may be, Larsen would know that once Lavinsky had his hands on the gold his life wouldn't be worth a mouldy biscuit.'

'Lavinsky will watch us,' observed Ginger.

'Of course, he will,' agreed Biggles. 'And for that reason I don't feel inclined to stay where he can see everything we do. That's been in the back of my mind all the time we've been talking; and I think I've got the answer. We'll move back to our old camp. The tent is still there, and enough stores to last for some time. Lavinsky would find it more difficult to watch us. He may think we've *gone*. If he does, so much the better, although I don't care much what he thinks. Another point is, the old camp lies to the east, and as the ice drift is that way we shouldn't have so far to fly when looking for Ginger's floe.'

'How do you intend to get the gold from the ice to the machine even if we find it?' asked Ginger. 'That's what beats me.'

'It beats me, too,' confessed Biggles. 'Of course, a lot would depend on where we found the floe — I mean, its position in relation to the main pack. If the floe has drifted a long way out to the sea we might as well go home, because the only thing that could get to it then would be a marine craft. I doubt if we could get one here in time to save it. The floe would start melting as soon as it came in contact with warmer air and water and the gold would finish at the bottom of the sea. But let's take one thing at a time. Our first job is to locate the gold.'

'Are you going to wait here for Algy to come?' asked the Skipper.

'I don't think so,' decided Biggles. 'There's no point in it. We might as well move now. We can make a signal to him when we're in the air and tell him we're moving a mile or two eastward. We'll make a good smoke; that will show him where we are. I was only hanging about here in the hope of getting a line on what Lavinsky intends to do — not that it's really important as long as he doesn't interfere with us. The only thing about that is, we ought to know what he's doing about Larsen. The wretched fellow must be got home somehow — but we'll deal with that later on. Let's get back to the old camp; Algy must be getting close.'

'What's Lavinsky going to think when he hears us start up?' asked Ginger.

'I've told you before I don't care what he thinks,' returned Biggles. 'If he was quite certain that we hadn't found the gold no doubt he'd be glad to see us out of his way. Let's get mobile.'

The roar of the motors brought Lavinsky and most of his crew to the rail of the *Svelt*, but they remained passive spectators as the aircraft swept across the snow field and into the air.

Visibility had improved somewhat, Ginger was relieved to find, but it was without success that he started towards the north in the hope of seeing the reserve machine approaching. The old camp was at once in view, and Biggles cruised towards it while Ginger went into the wireless compartment and sent a signal which he hoped would be picked up by Algy. This occupied only a few minutes, after which Biggles put the machine down without mishap, taxi-ing on and finally switching off close to the tent, which, with its contents, remained exactly as it had been left. Grimy attended to the skis while the Skipper melted snow for water to make tea. Biggles and Ginger employed themselves in marking out a landing T with old pieces of packing, and soon had a good black smoke rising from some oily rags.

The reserve machine arrived about ten minutes later. It circled once, losing height, and then came in to a smooth landing. Grimy took some more boards and slipped them under the skis. Presently Algy and Bertie climbed down and joined the party waiting for them on the ground.

'Here, I say, I hope you blighters haven't been keeping all the fun for yourselves,' greeted Bertie. 'Bit of a bind, sitting on that windy island with absolutely nothing to do.'

'We haven't had much fun so far,' Biggles told him. 'Gather round and grab a cup of tea while I give you the gen. And just remember we've got both machines here now, so if anything comes unstuck there's no one to take us off.'

'Why bring that up?' complained Bertie. 'I was trying to forget it.'

'What's that ship I noticed a mile or two along?' queried Algy.

'If you'll listen instead of asking questions I'll tell you all about it,' replied Biggles. Then, over mugs of steaming tea he narrated all that had happened since their arrival on the White Continent. 'That's how things stand at present,' he concluded. 'If anyone has a bright idea I'd be glad to hear it.'

No one answered for a little while. Then Bertie, who had been polishing his eyeglass thoughtfully, remarked: 'Deuced awkward — what?'

'I was hoping you'd appreciate that aspect,' answered Biggles, with gentle sarcasm.

'Absolutely — absolutely,' agreed Bertie. 'I'm all for getting after the jolly old gold. It's not every day a fella gets a chance to pick it up a ton at a time — no, by gad.'

'By the time you've picked up half of it you'll wish you'd never seen it,' promised Biggles. 'You two can have a rest and a cigarette while I have a look round. I'm making it a rule until we go for good that only one machine is in the air at a time, just in case of accidents, so don't go off on your own while I'm away. I'll take Ginger with me because he's the only one who has seen the particular piece of ice we're looking for.'

'Is there anything I can do?' asked the Skipper.

'Yes. You and Grimy can take turns watching the enemy camp. I don't think they'll try anything, but we should look silly if they did, and found us with no one on guard. There's a bit of a ridge a couple of hundred yards away; you can get a good view from the top of it.'

The Skipper nodded. 'Aye—aye. I know the one.'

Biggles glanced round the sky. 'The weather's still improving so let's go while the going's good.'

Within five minutes of the machine leaving the ground there occurred two events so unexpected that Ginger wondered for a moment if they could be true. Neither was really remarkable, being in the natural order of things, but they were startling in their unexpectedness. Whether or not Biggles thought they would find the gold Ginger did not know, but he himself took such a poor view of their chances that he did not even make a pretence of enthusiasm. Nor did he think seriously that the weather was improving. The temporary lifting of the cloud he took to be a mere passing phase, such as had occurred before. He was amazed therefore — not to say delighted — when, as if a curtain had been drawn aside, the cloud layer dispersed, leaving a flat mauve sky. The effect on the landscape was almost unbelievable. Visibility, from a few hundred yards, jumped to several miles. Ahead and on either side lay the deep blue water of the polar sea, dotted with a thousand glittering bergs and spreading floes. Astern stretched to the unknown hinterland of the White Continent, its southern horizon pierced by scores of mountains as yet unnamed, some rising to a tremendous height. As a spectacle, a spectacle that few men had seen, it was breath-taking.

Biggles' only remark was: 'That's better, now we can see what we're doing.'

But this was only a beginning. Happening to glance down, quite idly, a particular floe on account of its shape caught Ginger's eye, and held it. In an incredulous voice he shouted: 'There it is!'

Biggles looked at him. 'There what is?' he inquired.

'The floe we're looking for.'

Biggles astonishment was expressed in a frown. 'Are you sure?'

'Certain.'

'Where is it?'

Ginger pointed. 'That's it.'

'You're quite sure about it?'

'Well —' Ginger's eyes swept over the scores of floes visible from his altitude. There were, he noticed, several of similar shape, as the pieces of a jigsaw puzzle are similar, yet different. 'I'm pretty certain it's the one,' he declared. 'It's worth having a closer look at it, anyway.'

Biggles put the machine into a gentle turn, slowly losing height, while Ginger made a closer scrutiny of the floe. He could not see the stick, but that was hardly to be expected, because he realised that from his position above it, it would be foreshortened. And the ice-field was nearer to the shore than he had supposed it would be — less than a mile, he estimated. But the shape was right. Several other floes, presumably held by the same current, were close to it. Seaward, there was a wide stretch of open water. Beyond that again more floes were piling up in a wide arc; but these, he thought, were too far away to come within the same sphere of influence as the piece on which he had gone adrift.

'Take her a bit lower,' he requested. 'A side view may give me a sight of the stick. That's the only thing I can be really sure about.'

Biggles glided down towards the floe in question, lower and still lower, to flatten out eventually at about fifty feet. He then flew the whole length of the floe.

Suddenly Ginger let out a yell. 'That's it!' he shouted. 'I can see the stick. What a slice of cake.'

Biggles smiled. 'That's fine. We were about due to strike something easy for a change. Can you get an idea which way it's drifting.'

Ginger stared down for a minute or two. 'No,' he said at last. 'I don't think it's possible to tell from topsides; our own movement is too fast.'

'So I imagine,' returned Biggles. 'No matter. We'll go back. We shall be able to watch the ice from camp. We'll take a line on it from there. Keep your eyes on it or we may find ourselves watching the wrong one. I'm going in.'

'I won't lose sight of it, you can bet your life on that,' asserted Ginger warmly, as Biggles turned for home. Nor did he. Even when the aircraft landed his eyes were still on what must have been the most valuable piece of ice ever to float on the surface of the sea.

'What's the matter?' asked Algy, as they jumped down. 'I thought you'd be some time.'

'So did I,' answered Biggles. 'But it happens we've found the objective — took off straight over it. As soon as the sky cleared Ginger spotted it right away. If the sun will stay put and Lavinsky keep his distance the rest should be easy.'

'What are you going to do?' asked Algy.

'For the moment, nothing — nothing, that is, except watch that lump of ice to ascertain definitely which way it's drifting. A lot will depend on that.'

'Why not launch the jolly old dinghy — if you see what I mean,' suggested Bertie.

'And do what?'

'Bring home the boodle.'

'Have a heart,' protested Biggles. 'How long do you suppose it would take us to fetch the stuff a bar at a time? The dinghy wouldn't carry more. That floe is a mile away. Of course, if the worst comes to the worst we shall have to try it, but I don't relish the job. If that floe is drifting back towards the main pack, and I have an idea it is, if we have a little patience it will come to us. That will be a lot easier than fetching it — and safer. I'm not much for putting to sea on a piece of inflated rubber at the best of times. To spring a leak in this particular ditch wouldn't be funny.'

'Too true, old boy, too true. I'm with you there, absolutely,' declared Bertie. 'I like my water warm.'

'You'd find this definitely chilly, said Biggles grimly, as he picked up two trail sticks and arranged them in line with the floe. This done he sat behind the inner one, took a line through the other, and remained motionless for several minutes. 'It's coming in,' he announced, when at last he got up. 'I'll take another sight in a quarter of an hour. That should give us a rough idea of the rate of drift. This northerly breeze should help it. Meanwhile, we can occupy the time by having something to eat.'

CHAPTER 12

LAVINSKY SHOWS HIS HAND

By the end of half an hour, which had been occupied with eating a meal more satisfactory than savoury, it was evident that the floe carrying the gold was moving steadily towards the shore. The rate of drift was slow, but, Biggles thought, increasing under the influence of a rising breeze, which, fortunately, came from the right direction. The effect of this could be heard as well as seen, for there was an almost constant grinding and crunching of ice as the floes piled up together when their further progress was barred by the main ice shelf. The danger of employing the dinghy, or any craft for that matter, was now apparent.

'Lavinsky must be a fool, or else the gold has sent him stark raving mad,' asserted the Skipper once, as he watched with professional eyes the great masses of ice coming in. 'If that wind veers a point or two, and moves all that loose ice his way, he's had it, as you boys would say.'

'Well, I hope it doesn't,' said Biggles. 'Because if it does, and he loses his ship, we shall be expected to take him home.'

Biggles, too, had been watching the movement of the ice closely, and presently gave his opinion that the particular floe in which they were interested would, if its direction was maintained, come up against the ice-shelf not far from where they were waiting. There was some talk of trying to hoist a sail on the floe to hasten its progress; but the suggestion was not made seriously and was soon dismissed as impracticable. There was, therefore, nothing they could do except possess themselves in patience while they waited for the gold to come to them.

Lavinsky's movements were not ignored. Owing to the improved visibility it was now possible from the ridge near the camp to see the *Svelt.* Through binoculars it was also possible to see men moving about on the ice, some of them at a considerable distance from the ship. What they were doing, Biggles said he neither knew nor cared, as long as they kept out of the way. He supposed they were making a search either for the gold or the deranged Swede, who, Lavinsky may have thought, could tell them where it was. But when the report of a distant gunshot came through the crystal atmosphere Biggles frowned. 'What was that, I wonder,' he muttered.

'Probably shooting a seal,' answered the Skipper. 'Those fellows would kill anything for the sheer pleasure of doing it.'

'Perhaps you're right,' murmured Biggles, without conviction.

With irritating tardiness the floe crept nearer to the camp. With the aid of the glasses it was now possible to see not only Ginger's stick, but the slight hump of snow under which the gold lay hidden out of sight. Biggles sat on a packing case, smoking, until the nearest point of the ice was no more than a hundred yards distant; then he tossed the end of his cigarette aside and got up.

'We shan't be long now,' he remarked cheerfully. 'I've been thinking,' he went on. 'I'm going to load the reserve machine first. As soon as you've got a fair load aboard, Algy, you can fly it back to the Falklands.

You'll be empty except for the gold so you can take most of it. I'll follow you with the remainder and bring everyone back with me. There's no need for you to hang about here waiting for us.'

'Good enough,' agreed Algy. 'I think it's a good idea.'

The floe drifted nearer, and the whole party — with the exception of Grimy who was on guard at the ridge — went to the edge of the ice-shelf to wait for it. It could now be observed that the flat piece of ice, as well as drifting shoreward was also slowly turning, so that in the end it was the narrow part of the floe that first made contact with the mainland. Actually, this did not matter. It simply meant that they would have to walk a little farther to reach the gold. But as Biggles remarked, they had no cause for complaint; they were lucky that the floe had come ashore as close to the camp as it had.

At this stage of the proceedings Grimy returned at a run from his post to report that Lavinsky and six of his men were approaching.

Biggles sighed. 'They would choose this moment to come,' he muttered. 'We'd better not let them see what we're doing. We shall probably have trouble anyway, but we'll avoid it as long as we can. Don't let them see that we've any interest in that slice of ice or we might as well tell them what's on it.'

He sat down again on his packing case and lit a cigarette.

Lavinsky and his companions topped the ridge and came straight on to the camp, the leader a little in advance of the others. His expression was hostile, and when he opened the conversation he wasted no time in preamble. 'Where's that gold?' he demanded peremptorily.

Biggles regarded the speaker dispassionately. 'What

leads you to suppose that I know where it is?'

'I happen to know you know.'

Biggles' eyebrows went up. 'So what?' he inquired. 'What are you getting excited about, anyhow? The gold isn't yours.'

'It will be.'

'What you mean is, you hope it will be,' corrected Biggles. 'There's a difference,' he added.

'You said you hadn't got it,' rapped out Lavinsky.

'Perfectly true — I haven't.'

'That's a lie.'

Biggles smiled sadly. 'You're not such a smart guy after all, Lavinsky. If I'd got the gold what do you suppose I'd be doing here — sunbathing?'

Lavinsky hesitated, probably because the truth of Biggles' sarcastic observation was obvious. 'What have you done with it?' he challenged.

Biggles regarded him with a frown of disapproval. 'Who do you think you are that you can come into my camp and start slinging questions about? And what do you think I am that I should be likely to answer them? I'm trying to be patient with you, Lavinsky, but you're not making it easy. I'm the accredited agent of the British Government. Get that into your thick skull for a start. If anyone here has a right to ask questions it's me. As it happens there's no need. I know who you are and what we're doing here. I also know what happened on your last trip.'

'And I know you've got the gold,' almost spat Lavinsky.

'What makes you so sure of that?' asked Biggles curiously.

'Larsen told me. He watched you move it.'

'Ah! So you've found him?'

'Of course I found him.'

'The man's mad.'

'Not so mad that he didn't watch you find the gold and take it away.'

'He seems to have recovered somewhat since I last saw him,' murmured Biggles.

'I found a way to bring him to his senses.'

'Indeed?' Biggles' eyes narrowed. 'And just how did you achieve it?'

'Mind your own business.'

'This happens to be my business,' retorted Biggles with iron in his voice. 'You were responsible for his condition in the first place by abandoning him here. The least you can do now is get him home, although he'd probably be safer with me. Are you going to take him or shall I?'

'Bah! There's no need to worry about him.'

'Just what do you mean by that?' asked Biggles suspiciously.

Lavinsky's lips parted as if to answer, but he checked himself. 'If you want him you can have him,' he sneered.

'Had that gun shot I heard just now anything to do with him?' inquired Biggles, in an ominously brittle voice.

'Could have been.'

'Now you mark my words, Lavinsky,' said Biggles icily. 'The man was ill. You knew it. If you've injured him I'll see you pay for it. If you've killed him, then I'll do my best to see that you hang for it. Maybe you think you can get away with murder in a place like this. Well, you can't, as you'll discover in good time. Now get out of my camp before I throw you out.'

Lavinsky's manner changed, although for what

reason was not immediately apparent. 'All right, all right,' he muttered sulkily. 'That sort of talk won't get us anywhere.'

'I'll get you to the gallows if I have my way,' promised Biggles caustically.

Lavinsky's mollified tone was explained by his next suggestion. 'Look here, I'll tell you what I'll do,' said he. 'Gold's as useful to you as it is to me. You give me half of it and I'll clear out. You can have the rest. You can get a long way on half a ton of gold. That's fair enough, isn't it?'

'Your idea of fairness, Lavinsky, would make me laugh if the sight of you didn't make me feel sick,' answered Biggles contemptuously. 'I wouldn't give you one ounce even if I had it, which I haven't. Larsen was right when he saw us move it. Didn't he tell you where we put it?'

'Yes. He said you piled it up on the ice,' said Lavinsky eagerly.

'Didn't he tell you what happened to it after that?'

'No.'

'Would you like me to tell you?' Biggles seemed slightly amused.

'Sure.'

'It's still there.'

'What — where you put it?' Lavinsky's voice almost cracked with incredulity.

'Yes.'

'You mean — in the same place?'

'Well, not exactly,' answered Biggles. 'Larsen should have told you the rest of the story; but maybe he didn't know it. Anyway, as he didn't tell you, I will. And the only reason I'm telling you is to bring this futile argument to an end. I left a man on guard over the gold while I went off to fetch my machine. When I came back he wasn't there. What happened was, the particular area of ice chose that moment to break off. The man in charge didn't notice it until it was too late for him to do anything about it. He, and the gold, went adrift. You picked the man up — but not the gold. He was sitting on it. The gold is still on that same piece of ice. Now you know why I haven't got the gold and why I'm still here. Laugh that off and clear out — and stay out.'

If looks could kill Ginger would have been slain on the spot where he stood by the murderous scowl Lavinsky gave him. That he believed Biggles' story was not for a moment in doubt. It was so obviously true, not only from the way Biggles had told it but in his own experience. It explained exactly what must have been a puzzle to him all along. For a full minute he stood there staring malevolently from one to another. 'Okay,' he breathed at last. 'Okay, brother I'll get you yet — and the gold.'

'All you have to do is find the ice floe,' said Biggles smoothly.

'I'll do that,' said Lavinsky through his teeth. 'Before I go I'll give you a tip. Keep out of my way or you'll get what Larsen got. That goes for the lot of you.'

'I'll bear it in mind,' promised Biggles.

Lavinsky turned on his heels and calling to his men strode away.

Biggles and his party watched them go, Biggles smiling faintly, the others with mixed expressions. Not until Lavinsky and his companions had topped the ridge and disappeared from sight did anyone speak. Then the Skipper said: 'Why did you tell him that?'

'To get rid of him and gain time enough for us to finish the job. What I told him was obviously the truth, and he reacted just as I thought he would. By the time he's found the floe there'll be nothing on it — I hope. Anyway, had the man stayed here arguing the thing would have ended in shooting. I could see that coming — so could he. I decided it was better this way.'

'*Phew*,' breathed Ginger. 'You were taking a chance. I nearly broke into a perspiration every time the floe bumped against the shelf. I was expecting every minute he'd see that stick. That's twice he's had the gold under his nose without knowing it. He'll go raving mad when he realises it.'

'I shouldn't break my heart over that,' asserted Biggles. 'Let's get busy. The first thing is to get organised. The Skipper, Bertie and Grimy will haul the stuff here. Algy will help me to load up. Heavy stuff like gold can't just be chucked in anyhow. It will have to be distributed. Ginger, you'll take the glasses and watch Lavinsky. Let me know at once if he moves his ship or if you see any of his men coming this way. Let's get started.'

The work began, and for nearly an hour proceeded at full speed without interruption. By the end of that time about half of the gold had been moved to the aircraft. It was far from being a simple task, for a complication, a dangerous one, was caused by the constant movement of the ice floe against the solid pack. The floe did not, of course, fit flush against the main ice-shelf; it only made actual contact at one or two places, and even here the two masses sometimes swung apart leaving a gap too wide to be stepped across with safety. Again, there were times when the two masses came together with an alarming crash; on such occasions the splinters flew in all directions, at no small risk of injury to anyone who happened to be near the spot.

During this period, Ginger, who was on guard, made several reports to Biggles. First, he was able to announce that Lavinsky and his party had rejoined the ship. He next reported that the *Svelt* was on the move; it had left the pack-ice and was cruising about among the floes that littered the open water. As a matter of detail, Biggles had noticed this himself, for the ship was sometimes in view. It brought a smile to his face, for Lavinsky's purpose was fairly obvious. He was looking for the gold. After a while, however, the *Svelt* returned to its original mooring near the hulk. Ginger next reported that from time to time there was a brilliant flash of light from the crows-nest on the mainmast, although what caused this he was unable to say. Biggles being busy, paid little attention to it at the time. He was quite content that Lavinsky kept at a distance. Ginger's final report brought an end to the operation. Lavinsky, he said, was coming back, supported by a dozen men.

'I'm afraid that means war,' remarked Biggles. He looked across the floe at the remaining gold bars which, as the top ones had been removed, were conspicuous. 'We'd better not let him see that,' he went on, pointing to the gold. 'Grimy, slip out and cover the remainder up with snow; and as you come back you might brush some snow over the track we've made.'

While this was being done the Skipper questioned the advisability of waiting for what promised to be an attack in force, supporting his argument by pointing out that as they had half the gold they had reason to be satisfied.

'We can't take on that bunch and expect to get away with it,' he concluded, not without justification.

Biggles would not hear of it. 'I'm not leaving one bar, not half a bar, for that rascal,' he asserted. 'If we lose sight of the stuff we shall never find it again. Apart from that, I'm here on official business and refuse to be intimidated by that gang of sea-crooks.' He thought for a moment. 'I think we might compromise, though,' he resumed. 'We needn't risk losing the half we've already got. Algy, you might as well take it straight away to the Falklands. I shall have to ask you to go alone because if it comes to a rough house here, and things begin to look that way, I shall need as many hands as I can muster. If Lavinsky saw he had only two or three to deal with it might encourage him to try to wipe us out.'

'As you say, chief,' agreed Algy. 'I'll unload as fast as I can, refuel, and come straight back to help you with the rest. Otherwise, with the remainder of the gold and everyone else you look like being overloaded.'

'Fair enough,' agreed Biggles.

Ginger, who had been watching the advancing men, reported that they all seemed to be carrying weapons of some sort, guns or rifles.

Biggles shrugged. 'Two can play at that game.'

'Absolutely — absolutely,' murmured Bertie. 'I've promised to join Gimlet King for a spot of deer-stalking in the Highlands when I get back so I could do with a bit of practice. Pity the blighters haven't a decent head of antlers; I'd take one home to show Gimlet the sort of beasts we shoot in the lowest of the bally lowlands — if you see what I mean.'

'Lavinsky will get his horns in the next world, no doubt,' was Algy's parting remark as he walked over to his machine. In a minute or two he took off and headed out to sea.

Shortly afterwards Lavinsky and his supporters came into sight as they topped the ridge; and from the purposeful manner of their approach it was clear that the storm was about to break. Biggles took steps to meet it by telling the others to get weapons from the arms store, but warned them to keep them out of sight. He then placed them in strategical positions. So far there was nothing in the manner of Lavinsky's advance to suggest an immediate attack, but it was fairly evident that one might develop — particularly, as Biggles told the others, if the man thought he had them at a disadvantage.

Ginger seating himself behind a case of bully beef with a rifle across his knee, noticed that Algy, instead of carrying straight on his homeward course, had turned, and was now flying up and down as if engaged in a photographic survey of the area below him. Why he was doing this he could not imagine, and before he could arrive at a solution his attention was brought nearer to hand by Biggles calling out to Lavinsky not to come any closer. Lavinsky stopped at a distance of about ten yards with his men lined up on either side of him.

'Now what's biting you?' demanded Biggles curtly.

'You know why I've come here,' answered Lavinsky in a thin, rasping voice.

'Have you still got the gold bug in your brain?' enquired Biggles.

'Quit talking through your hat,' came back Lavinsky harshly. 'Thought you could fool me, eh. Well, think again, smart guy. I've been watching you from the mast through my glasses,' he added, thereby explaining the flashes that Ginger had reported. Apparently they had been caused by the sun catching the lens.

'I hope you enjoyed the picture,' replied Biggles evenly.

'The metal was here all the time. I saw you loading it up,' challenged Lavinsky.

'In that case you've nothing more to worry about,' answered Biggles. 'What you saw being loaded up is now on its way home.'

'Not all of it,' answered Lavinsky. 'I'll have the rest. Are you going to hand it over?'

'I most certainly am not.'

'Then I'll — ' Lavinsky glanced up as, with a roar, Algy's machine raced low over the camp. A small object hurtled down. Then the aircraft zoomed, turned and stood out to sea.

'Ginger, pick that thing up and see what it is,' ordered Biggles.

There was silence while Ginger ran to the object and brought it back. Biggles took it. It was a small cigarette tin, the sort to hold twenty cigarettes. He opened it and took out a slip of paper. He looked at it, smiled, rolled it into a ball and tossed the tin away. 'You were about to say something, Lavinsky, when we were interrupted,' he prompted.

'I was going to say that unless you hand over the metal I'm going to take it,' said Lavinsky viciously.

'And having got it — what then?'

Lavinsky hesitated for a moment as if he suspected that there was more behind Biggles' question than the mere words implied. 'I'll clear out and you can do what the hell you like,' he answered, his eyes on Biggles' face.

Biggles shook his head, 'You wouldn't get far, I'm afraid.'

'What do you mean by that? Do you reckon you could stop us?' Lavinsky grinned as if he found the idea amusing.

'If I didn't the ice would,' returned Biggles. 'Your ship's shut in. Between it and open water there's a half-mile-wide barrier of floes and bergs jammed together.'

Lavinsky's expression changed. 'Pah! You can't bluff me,' he answered; but there was no conviction in his voice.

Biggles raised a shoulder. 'Have it your own way.'

'How do you know?'

'You saw that message dropped a moment ago? The pilot is a friend of mine and he doesn't make mistakes. Please yourself whether you believe it or not. Personally, I couldn't care less.'

Ginger realised now the meaning of Algy's reconnaissance. The barrier could not be seen from where they were, but he spotted it from the air and realised its significance. So did Ginger. It put a new complexion on the entire situation. If the ice barrier did in fact prove impassable it looked as if the *Svelt* would share the fate of the *Starry Crown.* In that case they would be in the curious position of having to take Lavinsky and his crew home.

Lavinsky ran his tongue over his lips. He was probably thinking on the same lines, for Biggles was obviously telling the truth.

'It's no use standing there gaping at me,' resumed Biggles. 'I couldn't help you to get your ship clear even if I wanted to. Instead of yammering about getting the gold out you'd better see about getting yourselves out before it's too late. You can see which way the wind's blowing. That ice must be coming in this direction.

'It'll pack tighter, too, and get thicker as the reef shortens,' put in the Skipper. 'Once it closes in you and nips you, you're finished.'

Lavinsky's eyes wandered to the aircraft and then came back to Biggles. It was almost impossible to read his thoughts. 'If I stay you stay,' he snarled. 'I could soon shoot enough holes in that kite of yours, to keep it on the ground.'

'That would be really clever,' scoffed Biggles. 'Anyway, what do you suppose we should be doing while you were shooting?'

Lavinsky tried another tack. 'If we start shooting at each other we're all sunk,' he muttered, with a change of voice. 'There's no sense in that.'

'I was hoping that trivial point would occur to you,' returned Biggles.

'You wouldn't go off and leave me and the boys stranded here, I reckon?' There was a hint of anxiety in the question.

Biggles laughed shortly. 'Wouldn't I, by thunder! You don't know me. Why should I clutter myself up with a lot of useless scum that would be better in Davy Jones' locker? That's enough talking, Lavinsky. You're trapped. You've asked for it and you've got it. But because I've got a streak of weakness in me, if you'll obey my orders I'll give you a chance. You must have plenty of stores in your ship. Go back to it and stay there. There's a British naval sloop at the Falklands. As soon as I'm in the air I'll radio a signal and ask it to come here and take you off. Of course, I shall make a full report of what's happened here so you'd better be able to account for Larsen. That's as far as I'm prepared to go. Make up your mind what you're going to do, and make it up quickly. That's all.'

For a minute Lavinsky did not move. He glared at Biggles with hate smouldering in his eyes. Then, without another word he turned and strode away. His men followed, muttering among themselves. When he reached the ridge he stopped, and with his crew gathered round him, held what appeared to be a conference. It did not last long. Lavinsky and half a dozen men walked on towards the *Svelt*. The remainder sat down on the ridge facing the camp.

'So that's the game,' murmured Biggles.

CHAPTER 13

BIGGLES PLAYS FOR TIME

Biggles, sitting on a packing case, regarded the opposing force with thoughtful consideration.

'Well, old boy, what are we going to do about it — if you see what I mean?' inquired Bertie presently.

'I can see what you mean all right,' answered Biggles. 'I'm just trying to work it out.'

'What are those blighters doing, sitting on the hill?'

'Watching us.'

'But what joy will they get out of that?'

'None.'

'How long will they go on doing it?'

'As long as we don't make a move.'

'You mean, to load up the rest of the gold?'

'That's it.'

'But dash it all, we've as good as got it.'

'Yes, but not quite. Our problem is how to get the metal into the machine.'

'But is it as difficult as all that?'

'It's a lot more difficult than it looks,' asserted Biggles. 'Of course, there's a way out of difficulty; there always is. The problem is to find it — or, shall we say, the best way. By which I mean the safest way. Actually, there are several things we can do.'

Bertie looked disappointed. 'But look here, I don't get it. By telling that scallywag that the ice had put a cork in his bottle — if you see what I mean — I should have thought you'd have knocked his middle stump clean out of the ground.'

Biggles smiled lugubriously. 'Yes, you would think so,' answered Biggles. 'But I'm afraid he isn't the sort to accept the umpire's decision. He's got the gold fever too badly to listen to reason. He's going to get the gold, if he can, at any cost. If it would suit his book, in order to get it he'd bump us off without the slightest compunction. He's got a considerable force to back him up — and, in fact, he may have come here just now with that very object in view. But when he learned that he might have to depend on us to get him off the ice he had to think again. But that doesn't mean to say he's ready to pack up. Oh no.'

'But what can he do?' put in Ginger. 'It isn't likely that he's got an air pilot on board, so whatever happens he's bound to rely on one of us to get him home; and whoever did that would report him to the police as soon as his wheels touched the ground.'

'He isn't prepared to accept that — yet,' returned Biggles. 'I think what he's most likely to do next is confirm Algy's report that he's shut in. The fact that he's shut in now doesn't necessarily mean that he'll stay shut in. The ice may move again and give him a passage out, and he isn't likely to overlook that possibility. Even if that doesn't happen, as I see it he still has two chances of getting out. The first is to blast a gap through the ice with dynamite — I imagine he wouldn't come to this part of the world without any.'

'Quite right,' interposed the Skipper. 'We had dynamite on board when I had the ship.'

'His second resort, a more desperate one, might be to do what Last did. Last, you remember, fixed up a small boat, loaded it with stores and dragged it across the ice to open water — or at least he said he did, and I see no reason to disbelieve it. It was possible. And if it was possible for Last to do it single-handed, Lavinsky, with several boats to choose from and twenty men to handle them, should have no great difficulty in doing it. My guess is that he's gone off to have a dekko. If he decides he can get out he'll come back here with all hands to try to wipe us out.'

'But he couldn't do that without getting some of his own men knocked out,' protested Ginger.

'Huh! That wouldn't be likely to worry him as long as he escaped himself,' replied Biggles.

'But half a minute, old boy, what's come over you?' cried Bertie. 'It isn't like you to talk as if Lavinsky and his thugs have only to come here and pop off a gun for us all to drop dead. He wouldn't get us as easy as that — no, by gad.'

'There are times, Bertie, when I think you must be sheer bone from one ear to the other,' said Biggles sadly. 'I'm not worried overmuch about Lavinsky shooting at *us*, as individuals. It would be easier to hit the aircraft, and there's nothing we can do to prevent that. We can't put the machine under cover. He has only to put a few holes through the tanks and we shall be the ones to stay here, not him. He knows that, too. My talk just now to Lavinsky, about him being stuck here, was mostly bluff. Lavinsky may not have seen through it at the time, but when he's thought the matter over, he will. He just wants to confirm that he can't get out before he takes steps to make sure that we can't. Of course, if he decides he's caught in the ice, good and proper, he'll have to rely on us to get him out, whether he likes it or not.'

'Hadn't we better push off while the going's good?' suggested the Skipper tentatively.

'And leave that rascal the gold? Not on your life,'

Biggles was emphatic.

'Then let's get the gold on board and take it with us,' suggested Ginger. 'I'm getting cold sitting here.'

'The moment we make a move towards that gold the fireworks will start,' answered Biggles. 'Now you all know why I'm apparently content to sit here and do nothing. Give me a minute and I may work the thing out.'

Nothing more was said. Biggles lit another cigarette. Ginger gazed moodily across the waste of snow, now pink in the glow of a westering sun. It struck him as odd that even here a mere handful of men could not exist without threats of violence. No wonder, he mused, all over the civilised world the atmosphere was brittle with fears and threats of war.

Presently he broke the silence. 'Suppose Lavinsky got away in his boats, where would he go?' he questioned. 'He's a long way from anywhere.'

The Skipper answered. 'He'd have no great difficulty in getting to South America — unless he ran into heavy seas. He's got plenty of stores. Longer trips than that have been made in open boats, many a time, and will be made again, no doubt.'

There was another silence. This time it was broken by Bertie. He stood up and buffed his arms. 'Well, what are we going to do, old boy?' he asked. 'This doing nothing is binding me rigid. It's beastly cold.'

Biggles drew a deep breath. 'Yes, I suppose we might as well do something,' he agreed. 'Let's see if we can get the gold on board. That may stir the enemy into action, anyway. I'm afraid it's going to be a longish job.'

Ginger looked at Biggles. 'You think that'll be the signal for the enemy to open fire on us.'

'I'm pretty sure of it. For what other reason would

Lavinsky leave six men on the ridge? If it was just to watch us, one would have been enough.'

'If we can't get the stuff on board we could at least push off,' said Bertie cheerfully.

'You seem to be forgetting something,' remarked Biggles.

'What's that?'

'Larsen. The idea of leaving the wretched fellow here goes against the grain. But there, we'll talk about that when we've got the gold.'

'If they start shooting at us I reckon we can shoot back,' put in the Skipper grimly.

'I reckon we can,' agreed Biggles. 'Our difficulty would be to fight a gun battle and transport the gold here at the same time. We could do it, maybe, but it would be a slow business. Anyhow, let's try it and see what happens. Skipper, you're the strongest man in the party. Suppose you try fetching a bar while we keep you covered. If anything starts, drop the gold and make back for here.' He smiled faintly. 'When the enemy realises what you're doing it will be interesting to see whether they fire at you or at the aircraft. At any rate, that should tell us what Lavinsky's orders were to the men he left there.'

'Why not let me take the aircraft off the ground and cruise around while the shooting goes on?' proposed Bertie.

Biggles shook his head. 'I thought of that. We can't afford the petrol, and it would come to the same thing in the end, anyway. The machine would have to land to pick up the gold. Let's get the stuff here for a start. We needn't load it up. We could soon do that once it's here. If things get too hot, we shall have to pack up, of course. This is no place to have casualties.' Biggles reached for his binoculars and focused them on the *Svelt*. 'I wasn't far wrong,' he observed presently. 'They've lowered a lifeboat. It's on its way to the ice barrier. Okay, Skipper. Go ahead and fetch an ingot. If trouble starts, drop it and make for home.'

'Aye — aye, sir.' The Skipper set off across the ice.

That the move was noticed by the enemy was at once apparent, for they had been sitting down, and now stood up to watch. One set off at a fast pace in the direction of the *Svelt*.

'He's going to report to the boss,' conjectured Biggles.

The remaining five men, after a short discussion, disappeared from sight behind the ridge. But not for long. One by one their heads reappeared and weapons were now in evidence. A shot rang out, and a bullet flicked up some snow fairly wide of the Skipper, who, however, carried on.

'What's he doing?' muttered Biggles. 'I told him to come back if shooting started.'

'He won't come back until he's got what he went for,' asserted Grimy. 'I know my old man.'

Biggles spoke quietly. 'It's a tricky light for shooting, and shooting over snow is always deceptive; but I don't want anybody hit, so we've got to get those fellows off that ridge. The best way to do that is by enfilading them. Bertie, keep low and see if you can work your way to the end of their line. If you can do that you ought to be able to make things uncomfortable for them. Meanwhile, we'll try to make them keep their heads down from here.'

Another shot rang out from the ridge. Another feather of snow leapt up near the Skipper, who ignored it.

'Okay,' said Biggles grimly. 'If that's how they want it they can have it. Take what cover you can everybody and open fire. Don't waste ammunition. Pick your man and shoot low.'

Biggles settled himself behind the case on which he had been sitting, and taking careful aim, fired.

The man who had been his target ducked, but there was no spurt of snow to mark where the bullet had struck. 'I think I was over him,' Biggles told the others. 'Try shooting a foot below the target.' He fired again. The head at which he had aimed disappeared, but whether or not the man had been hit there was no means of knowing.

By this time Ginger and Grimy were also shooting, with the result that the heads lining the ridge no longer remained still. Only occasionally did one show, and then for not more than a second.

'I don't think they're in love with their job,' remarked Biggles. 'Hold your fire until you see something to shoot at. As long as we can make them keep their heads down the Skipper can carry on.'

Firing continued in a desultory manner.

Presently the Skipper came back, puffing, with an ingot on his shoulder.

'Nice work, Skipper,' complimented Biggles. 'Dump it near the machine — somewhere handy for the cabin door. I think we've got the situation pretty well in hand. Feel like fetching another?'

'There's nothing to it,' answered the Skipper, grinning, and set off again across the ice.

Biggles, with his rifle at the ready, watched the ridge. From time to time a head would pop up and a shot would be fired, but in such haste that the bullet usually went wide.

Presently the Skipper came back with another bar. Without waiting for an order he dropped it beside the first and set off again across the ice.

For a while there was a certain amount of sporadic shooting. Then Bertie was heard in action at the far end of the line. There was a brisk burst of shots, then the shooting died away altogether.

'I think we've got superiority of fire, as they say in the army,' opined Biggles. 'Grimy, go and help your father. Ginger, I think you might as well go too. I'll hold the fort. If anything serious starts, drop everything and come back at the double.'

Ginger and Grimy put down their weapons and went off at a run.

Thereafter, for about an hour, there was no change in the situation. Not for a moment did Biggles take his eyes off the ridge. The stack of ingots near the aircraft grew steadily. But this satisfactory state of affairs came to an end when Ginger, on one of his homeward trips, shouted to Biggles that the enemy was receiving reinforcements. A boat was on its way across the open water.

Biggles snatched a glance. Out over the sea, beyond the floe on which the others were working, was the lifeboat. It was plain to see what was happening. Lavinsky, apparently, had made his survey of the ice reef, and having heard the shooting, instead of returning to the *Svelt* was making straight towards the floe from which the gold was being recovered, with the obvious intention of landing on it. By doing this he was saving himself a considerable amount of time. Biggles had relied on this time to finish the job he had started, but it was now evident that it would not work out that way. Another twenty minutes would see Lavinsky and his party on the floe. Not only would that put an end to any further work on it, but, what was far more serious, it would put the camp between two fires. If Lavinsky had found a way through the ice barrier, reasoned Biggles, he would first rush the remainder of the gold and then concentrate his fire on the aircraft. A target of such size could hardly be missed. Once the machine was out of action Lavinsky could pretty well finish things in his own time.

Biggles acted swiftly. To Ginger he shouted: 'How many ingots are there left?'

'About half a dozen,' was the answer.

'All right. Leave it at that,' ordered Biggles. 'Start stowing the stuff in the machine.' He gave the Skipper and his son the same order when they returned.

No shots had yet been fired from the approaching boat, possibly because the movement of it would make anything like accurate shooting impossible; but Biggles realised that as soon as the men were on firm ice the camp would quickly become untenable. At this juncture Bertie reappeared to report that what looked like the remainder of the ship's company — he had counted seven — were hurrying towards the scene with the apparent object of reinforcing those behind the ridge. These, Bertie, said, he had driven to the far end of the ridge where they had found cover behind some broken ice.

Biggles counted aloud. 'Seven. There are six in the boat. That makes eighteen all told.' Turning to the Skipper who was now helping to load the gold he called: 'How many hands had you in the *Svelt*?'

'Nineteen,' was the answer.

'Did that include you and Lavinsky?'

'No.'

'Then it looks as if he's got nearly everybody here.'

The Skipper paused in his work to answer. 'He might as well have them here; there's nothing for them to do on the ship. If they've left anyone it'll be the cook. He's a Chinese, and a very old man at that—that's if he's the man who sailed under me. He's deaf, too.'

'Good,' replied Biggles. 'Buck up and get that gold stowed.'

'What are you going to do?' asked the Skipper. 'This is going to be a hot spot presently.'

'I'm going to fly down to the *Svelt*,' Biggles startled everyone by saying.

'What in blazes for?' demanded the Skipper, obviously shaken by a move so unexpected.

'The breeze is off-shore where she lies,' answered Biggles. 'I imagine Lavinsky will have made her fast with cables fore and aft.'

'That's what I should do.'

'Then if we cut free she'll drift away from the main pack.'

The Skipper looked aghast at the idea. 'But you can't cast away a ship like that,' he cried.

'You'd be surprised at the things I can do,' replied Biggles grimly. 'Lavinsky is done if he loses his ship. When he sees she's adrift he'll have to lay off what he's doing and go back to save her.'

The Skipper grinned. 'You're right! So he will.'

'I'm playing for time,' said Biggles. 'Look lively with that gold and we'll get cracking. There's nothing like giving the enemy something he doesn't expect.'

There was a little more shooting whilst the rest of the gold was being stowed, but the range was long, and as far as could be seen the shots did no damage. By this time Lavinsky's boat had reached the far side of the floe, at a point about two hundred yards from the gold, and was making ready to disembark on the ice.

'Why not push off altogether?' asked Ginger. 'We've got practically all the gold.'

'I'm not thinking entirely of the gold,' returned Biggles tersely. 'Have you forgotten Larsen? He may be dead, but there's a chance that he's still alive, possibly wounded. I shouldn't sleep comfortably in my bed again if I thought we'd left him to the tender mercies of this ship-rat, Lavinsky. As I say, he may have killed him; but if he hasn't he will. He's not likely to take home someone who could stand as a witness against him.'

With that Biggles climbed into his seat and started up. The others got aboard. Ginger, looking through a side window, remarked that the boat's crew was no longer hurrying.

'They think we're going home,' said Biggles. 'They'll move fast enough when they spot their mistake, I'll warrant.'

CHAPTER 14

WAR ON THE ICE

Biggles took off without trouble, and after climbing to a safe height came round in a wide turn. From the air the scene below became contracted into a small area and it was possible to see every member of the enemy forces. Those in the boat had stopped what they were doing to stare upwards as the machine passed over them. Tiny spurts of smoke revealed that shots were being fired, but at such an extreme range and at such a fast-moving target, there was, Ginger thought, no cause for uneasiness.

Biggles paid no heed to those below. His big concern was to put the heavily-loaded aircraft down without damage. In the ordinary way he would not have given such a routine operation a second thought, but so much now depended on the machine remaining airworthy that what would normally be a molehill of anxiety now looked like a mountain. Everyone realised this, and no one moved or spoke as Biggles brought the machine round in a cautious approach. However, all went well, and Ginger drew a long breath of relief as the machine skidded to a standstill about two hundred yards from the *Svelt*. Not a soul appeared on deck, nor was there any sign of life in the vicinity.

Grimy, who had brought some boards with him, jumped down and slipped them under the skis. The others were soon out, and Biggles advanced quickly towards the ship, which, as had been anticipated, was moored fore and aft to steel pins driven into the ice. The Skipper took out his knife and moved towards the nearest rope. Biggles stopped him. 'Just a minute,' he said. 'I'm going to see if Larsen is in that ship. Lavinsky must have spoken the truth when he said he'd found him, otherwise he wouldn't have known about the gold; and I don't know where else he could be. You know your way about the ship, Skipper, so you'd better come with me. Ginger, you follow behind and guard our rear, just in case someone is hiding and tries to pull a fast one on us. Bertie, you'll stay here and keep an eye on things.'

There was still no sign of life on the ship so it did really seem as if the entire crew had gone ashore. A rope ladder hung over the side down to the firm ice. Biggles went up it quickly and stood looking about until the Skipper and Ginger had joined him.

'Anyone at home?' called Biggles sharply.

There was no answer.

Biggles walked on to the companion-way, but before going below he stopped to gaze across the water in the direction of Lavinsky's boat, which, being at the outer edge of the floe, could be seen beyond a projecting ice-cliff. Ginger looked, too, and smiled as he saw that the men who had disembarked were now back in the boat, which, judging from the flash of oars, was making back for the *Svelt* at top speed.

Biggles laughed softly. 'If we've done nothing else we've given Lavinsky a fright,' he observed. 'No doubt he thinks we're about to set fire to the ship and leave him here — and it would serve him right if we did. But let's go below. You lead the way Skipper. You'll know where to look for Larsen if he's here.'

The Skipper now took the lead. 'Aye. I reckon I know

where he'll be, if he isn't dead and under the ice,' he agreed, as they reached the foot of the steps. 'Stand fast while I go and look. There's no need for everyone to go.' He strode on and disappeared from sight.

He was away about five minutes. When he came back his face was pale with anger. 'Just as I thought,' he said in a hard voice. 'They'd put him in irons.'

'What about the key?' asked Biggles quickly.

'I've got it. I found it in Lavinsky's cabin. Let's go and get him out.'

'How does he seem?'

'Quiet as a lamb, no wonder,' replied the Skipper grimly. 'He's been wounded, and he's half dead from loss of blood. His shirt's stiff with gore. As near as I can make out he got a bullet just under the shoulder. He's in a pretty mess, one way and another.'

Biggles drew a deep breath. 'Okay,' he said quietly. Let's get him up. We'll take him straight to the aircraft and fly him home. Ginger, you stay here and watch the passage in case of accidents. Lead on Skipper.'

Ginger took out his pistol and remained where he was while the others went on. He had not long to wait. Very soon they reappeared, half carrying, half supporting a body that looked more dead than alive. Ginger did not stop to look at the unfortunate sailor closely, but taking the lead went back to the deck.

It took all hands to get the helpless Swede down to the ice, for although he was emaciated he had a big frame, and the heavy clothing he wore would alone have made a load. However, the job was done and the man carried half way to the aircraft. Then Biggles called a halt while the Skipper went back to cut the *Svelt* adrift. This did not take long, for the vessel, with an off-shore breeze on her quarter, was already straining gently at her mooring ropes. The Skipper did some quick work with his knife and the ship was free. She began at once to move slowly away from the ice.

'That should give Lavinsky something to think about,' observed Biggles with satisfaction, looking in the direction of the boat, which was now about half way to the ship.

The shore party, Ginger noticed, were also about half way, strung out like runners at the end of a long race.

'We ought to be away before they get here,' said Biggles. 'Come on, let's keep going.'

The transportation of the sick Swede to the aircraft was continued, and in a little while he was made comfortable on a bed of blankets on the floor of the cabin.

'Now let's see what we can do for him in the way of first aid, or he looks like passing out before we can get him to the Falklands,' said Biggles. 'I think we've got time.'

The medicine chest was produced, and Biggles was opening it when he paused, sniffing the air. 'Can I smell petrol?' he asked sharply, a quick frown lining his forehead.

There was a brief silence. Then Ginger answered: 'Yes, I think you can.'

'See if you can locate it,' ordered Biggles.

Ginger went off while Biggles, with the Skipper's assistance, set to work on the wounded man. The wound, it was soon discovered, had not even been bandaged.

When Ginger came back it was with the bad news that the rear main tank had been holed by a bullet, fortunately by one of small calibre. A little petrol had been lost, but not much. 'I've plugged the hole in the meantime with a piece of chewing gum,' he stated.

For a moment nobody spoke. Then, without looking up from his patient, Biggles said: 'You'll have to get that hole properly plugged.

'All right, but it'll take time. I doubt if it's possible to do it before Lavinsky gets here.'

'That's awkward,' murmured Biggles. 'Still, there's nothing else for it. We shall need every drop of petrol, and I'm not starting on nearly a thousand miles of open sea with a leaky tank. Just a minute, though.' Biggles stopped work and looked up. 'It's no use staying here,' he went on. 'Once Lavinsky gets within range he'll put holes in our tanks a lot faster than we can mend them. There's only one thing we can do. As soon as Lavinsky and the shore party get close enough to be dangerous we'll fly back to the original camp and do the job there. It's a confounded nuisance, but I can't think of any other way. There is this about it, if it's any comfort to you; if we're tired of this shuttlecocking to and fro, Lavinsky's gang, who have to do it on their feet, must be even more fed up with it. Lavinsky will have to secure his ship before he can come after us again, anyway, and that will take time. We should have two or three hours clear while he's getting to her, bringing her back and making her fast, and then marching back to us — if he decides to do that. By that time his men will need a rest, too. We could pick up the remainder of the gold while we're waiting for Ginger to fix the tank.'

'There's only one thing about that,' answered Ginger slowly. 'I've just had a look at the barometer. It's falling fast. It's perishing cold, and getting colder.'

'Aye,' put in the Skipper. 'There's a change on the way. I can feel it.'

Biggles looked at Ginger. 'Make a start on that hole,'

he ordered. 'Skipper, you watch the weather. Bertie, keep an eye on the enemy. I've plenty to do here.' He carried on with his first aid work. Larsen, Ginger noticed as he turned away, had lapsed into unconsciousness.

It was nearly an hour later, as Biggles was tidying up, that Bertie reported that Lavinsky had reached and boarded the *Svelt*. The nearest members of the shore party were only about five hundred yards away. They were coming on, but very slowly, as if they were tired.

'Okay,' acknowledged Biggles. 'We'll push along. Shut the door.' He went through to the cockpit, started the engines, and having given them a minute or two to warm up, took off, heading once more for the old camp. Reaching it he made a circuit, watching the ground closely to make sure that the enemy had all gone, before landing along his original track. 'Get busy everybody,' he called, when he had switched off. 'Ginger, get that hole properly plugged. Do the job well. We can't take chances. The rest of you bring in what's left of the gold while I knock up some hot grub.' He jumped down and looked at the sky, now overcast again. His breath hung round him like bonfire smoke.

The loading of the gold was finished inside an hour, during which time the weather slowly deteriorated. But Ginger's task took longer, although Grimy went to his assistance. The trouble, as he told Biggles, was the bitter cold. It was intense. He could not work with gloves on — at least not very well — and yet it was dangerous to take them off, for the risk of frost-bite was obvious. Any metal touched seemed to burn. Bare fingers stuck to it, leaving the skin adhering after a minute or two. Ginger had to stop repeatedly to beat his hands together to keep the circulation going. Two hours later, although desperately tired, he was still at it. Biggles took him some hot coffee.

Meanwhile, the enemy had not been idle. Lavinsky had reorganised his forces for what was clearly a last desperate attempt to get the gold. The *Svelt*, now under control, had gone first to the ice shelf to pick up the men who had been left ashore. Now, under full power, it was heading for the camp, at no small risk, as the Skipper pointed out, of tearing its keel off on one of the many pieces of ice that covered the water. In this respect, however, Lavinsky's luck was in, and the *Svelt* ploughed on its way unharmed. That Lavinsky intended to launch a general attack on the aircraft from two directions became plain when, at a distance of about half a mile, he brought his ship alongside the ice and put ashore a dozen men armed with rifles. These at once fanned out in a wide semi-circle before advancing towards the camp. The *Svelt* then came on towards the far side of the floe from which the remaining ingots of gold had been removed. On this field of ice more of the ship's company were landed, and under the leadership of Lavinsky himself came on in open order towards the machine.

'This is going to be a warm spot presently,' remarked the Skipper, buffing his arms. 'As soon as they're in range the fun will start.'

At this point of the proceedings Ginger announced that his job was done. The tank was okay.

'Just in time,' returned Biggles. 'We'd better be moving.'

'Absolutely, by Jove. I was beginning to get worried,' murmured Bertie. 'Beastly cold sitting here doing nothing.'

Biggles went through to the cockpit to start up.

Ginger took his place at the second pilot's seat. The port engine started, but the starboard one remained silent. Biggles tried again. Nothing happened. He glanced at Ginger. 'She's cold,' said he, and tried again. But the engine was obstinate and remained dead. 'No use,' said Biggles. He had one more try. It failed. 'How very annoying of it,' muttered Biggles. 'Get the heater.'

Ginger looked aghast. 'But while we're fiddling with that Lavinsky will arrive,' he cried.

Biggles shrugged his shoulders. 'So what? I can't get her off on one engine.'

'The temperature was twenty-eight below zero the last time I looked at the thermometer,' said Ginger morosely.

'We should have done something about it before,' stated Biggles. 'Being busy I didn't realise it was as cold as that. Still, it's no use talking about that. We've got to warm that motor before it'll start so we might as well get at it. You handle it. I'll try to keep Lavinsky at a distance.'

Ginger felt sick at heart. That they should find themselves grounded at this most critical moment was maddening, but, as Biggles had said, there was only one thing they could do about it. He climbed out of his seat and adjusted the heating apparatus which had been installed for that purpose. How long it would take to operate he did not know, but several minutes at least would be required.

A shot rang out, and, simultaneously a bullet struck the machine somewhere. Not being quite ready for it, Ginger jumped. Biggles, he thought, had not been far wrong. This was a clear indication of what they could expect.

Another shot cracked in the brittle atmosphere, but

this, Ginger saw, had been fired by Biggles at the enemy advancing across the ice-floe. Shots came back, Lavinsky's men shooting as they walked. Bertie also fired, but as far as Ginger could see, without effect. This non-effective shooting, by people whom he knew to be first-class shots, was, he thought, one of the most surprising things of the expedition. He could only assume that it was due to the peculiar white light. Everything was white, the sky as well as the ground. A little breeze moaned mournfully across the frozen sterility and the penetrating cold of it brought tears to his eyes. It seemed the height of lunacy to go on fighting in such conditions, for the wind or snow — or both, as seemed likely — promised to put an end to both expeditions. Whichever side won would be lucky to get away with their lives. But apparently Lavinsky in his gold madness cared nothing for the consequences of what he was doing. More shots were exchanged. It was obvious that someone presently would be hit. Both sides could not go on missing. The range was getting shorter.

Biggles must have realised this, too, for his face was drawn with anxiety when he shouted to Ginger to start up as soon as this was possible. Ginger moved to give the recalcitrant engine another trial. But, even as he did so, a shot whistled past him to stop with that curious 'phut' which a bullet makes when it strikes flesh. Snatching a glance over his shoulder he saw Grimy sink down in the snow and then try to rise, clutching at his left arm.

'Grimy's hit,' he shouted to Biggles.

'Get him inside and do what you can for him,' answered Biggles, punctuating his words with shots. '*And get that engine going.*'

Ginger helped Grimy into the aircraft where a quick examination revealed that the wound was not serious — or at any rate it would not have been considered serious in a temperate climate. The bullet had passed through the muscle of the upper arm, lacerating it badly. Ginger clapped on a pad and bound it on with some haste, for the rattle of musketry outside made it clear that the battle was nearing its climax. Several bullets struck the machine, but as far as he could ascertain from a quick inspection, without serious damage. Perceiving that their only hope now was to get the engine started he was on his way to try it when a fresh complication arose. From overhead came the vibrant drone of a low-flying aircraft.

Ginger knew that this could only be Algy, who had now returned as he had promised. In the excitement he had forgotten all about him. It seemed highly improbable that Algy would realise what was going on below him, and Ginger's heart sank as he perceived that, far from the machine serving any useful purpose. Algy would merely land with fatal results to himself. One man more or less could make no difference to the result of the one-sided battle.

Biggles realised this, too, of course, and as Ginger jumped down he shouted to him to try to signal to Algy to keep out of it, he himself being busily engaged in trying to keep Lavinsky's men from getting any nearer. Just how Algy was to be prevented from landing Ginger did not know, for the machine was already circling preparatory to coming in. All Ginger could do was run out waving his arms wildly, but for all the effect this had he might as well have remained under cover instead of exposing himself to the enemy, some of whose shots whistled unpleasantly close.

Ginger groaned as, with no more concern than if it had been up on a test flight, the Wellington glided in to a perfect landing. And as if that were not enough, thought Ginger, with a sinking feeling in the stomach, it must needs finish its run right in front of those members of Lavinsky's crew who were closing in from the landward side. Instinctively Ginger yelled a warning although he knew quite well that it could not be heard. But it was all he could do, except run towards the plane firing past it with his automatic at some men who had jumped up and were making towards it. One of them fell, but the rest ran on, shouting triumphantly, as if delighted at having made such an important capture. If that was their opinion Ginger shared it, and he fully expected to see Algy shot dead the moment he showed himself. But to his stupefaction it was not Algy who sprang out, but a naval officer; and behind him, as if impelled by some hidden mechanism, came bluejackets, faster than Ginger could count. The effect was electrical. Ginger stopped staring, making incoherent noises. Lavinsky's men stopped, too, which was no matter for wonder. They wavered in indecision, and without firing another shot retired precipitately, some throwing away their weapons. Thus might hooligans have fled on the arrival of a squad of policemen.

In a flash the whole situation was changed, and without another weapon being fired; for even Lavinsky, finding himself confronted by authority in a form which it is not wise to provoke, made off towards the *Svelt*, thinking perhaps that if he could get his ship clear of the ice he would be safe from pursuit — for the time being at any rate.

The bluejackets started after the attackers who had now become fugitives, but Biggles ran out and called to the officer to stop them.

'I don't think you need break your necks chasing that bunch,' Biggles told him, as he came up. 'They can't get far. They're the wrong side of the ice barrier. You can come back and pick them up later on — or you can leave them where they are as far as I'm concerned. I want to get out of this before the weather closes in on me. I don't like the look of it. I've got wounded men to get home, anyway, so the sooner we're off the better. I've got what I came for. Much obliged to you for coming to give us a hand.' Turning to Algy he concluded: 'You timed that very nicely; things were getting serious.'

'I had an idea they might be,' answered Algy. 'So did the Senior Naval Officer at Falklands Station when I told him what was afoot and who was here. Apparently he knows Lavinsky by reputation as a seal poacher, and a bad hat altogether, so he suggested that instead of flying back empty I brought these fellows along to tidy the place up.'

The naval officer glanced round the sky. 'I think you're right about getting back,' he agreed. 'Lavinsky can't do much harm here now and we can always pick him up when it suits us. The Old Man will probably send a sloop down for him.'

'That's fine,' concurred Biggles. 'Let's divide the load and set a course for home before we all get chilblains.'

There was a general move towards the machines.

CHAPTER 15

THE END OF THE STORY

The rest of the story is soon told. The two Wellingtons returned together without incident to the Falklands Islands, where Grimy and Larsen at once received proper medical attention. Biggles straightway made a signal home through official channels reporting the success of the expedition, and this promptly brought a reply to the effect that the airmen were to make their own way home in their own time, leaving the gold to be brought back by one of H.M. ships. This decision, which relieved Biggles of any further responsibility in the matter, suited him very well. As he remarked to the others, the machines would fly better without so much dead weight, and he, at all events, had already seen enough of it. Gold, he asserted, always meant trouble. It always had, and probably always would. The thing now was to forget about it.

After a week's rest, and a top overhaul of the machines, the expedition returned home, following the route it had taken on the outward passage. Grimy, his arm in a sling, went with it, but Larsen, still being too ill to travel, was left behind.

Some time elapsed before any news came through about Lavinsky and his crew. There was, however, a good reason for this. No news was available, for following the departure of the expedition from the Antarctic came a succession of gales so severe that any attempt to reach the men would have been not only dangerous but futile. So they had remained where they were for the long polar winter. When, the following season, a Falklands Islands Dependencies sloop reached the spot only eleven men remained alive. Lavinsky was not among them, nor were his owners, Shim and Sham. The story told by the survivors was probably true in the main, although naturally, all the blame for what had happened was piled on those who had died. The *Svelt*, it appeared, had not been able to get out, and was eventually frozen in the ice. The crew, of course, had continued to live in the ship. The result, considering the number and type of men, was inevitable. There had been quarrels, and in the end, open fighting. In one of these brawls Lavinsky had been shot by a man who had subsequently died; but who had actually killed him was never discovered.

At the trial, which came later on a charge of seal poaching, one of the men, to save himself, had turned King's Evidence; and he stated, probably with truth, that Lavinsky's behaviour had become so brutal that a conspiracy was formed to put him off the ship, and this had resulted in shooting, in which Lavinsky and his partisans, which included men known as Shim and Sham, had been killed. What actually happened during that dreadful period will probably never be known. Anyway, those who were brought home merely exchanged one prison for another.

In due course the gold arrived at the Bank of England and after some delay the salvage money, as arranged, was paid to those by whose efforts the gold had been recovered. After a final dinner together the Skipper and his son returned to Glasgow, where the Skipper bought a house overlooking his home port, and Grimy acquired a motor business which is now flourishing.

The comrades, after a short leave, returned to routine duty, which, as Bertie observed, while dull, did at least permit them to have a hot bath when they felt like it.

It was some time before anything was heard of Larsen and it was feared that he must have died. Then, one day, a letter arrived from the man himself. In it he told Biggles that he had so far recovered that he was able to join a Norwegian whaler that had put in at Port Stanley. The purpose of the letter was to convey his gratitude for his salvation from a horrible fate, but in closing he mentioned a detail which, in the haste to depart from the White Continent, had been overlooked at the time. This was the bar of gold that he had seized when he had first bolted from the hulk. He said he remembered the incident quite well. He had hidden the gold under some ice. He had not mentioned the existence of it to Lavinsky so only he knew where it was. It was still there.

'And as far as I'm concerned,' remarked Biggles, as he folded the letter, 'it can stay there,'

'Absolutely, old boy, absolutely,' agreed Bertie warmly. 'I'm with you every time. There's no future in icebergs — if you see what I mean.

'I've got a fair idea of what you mean,' admitted Biggles, smiling.

If you have enjoyed this book, you may like to read some more thrilling Biggles adventures published by Knight Books:

BIGGLES MAKES ENDS MEET

CAPTAIN W. E. JOHNS

Biggles and his friends are investigating a complaint of 'armed robbery on the high seas', but they soon realised that they are dealing with much more than simple piracy. Instead they have stumbled upon a vast and hitherto well-concealed drug smuggling ring.

The search for the ring-leaders and their secret island headquarters leads Biggles across the vast expanses of the Indian Ocean. He's up against powerful and desperate men, and if that's not enough he's heading straight into a monsoon!

KNIGHT BOOKS

BIGGLES AND THE NOBLE LORD

CAPTAIN W. E. JOHNS

When Biggles sets out to investigate a series of brilliantly masterminded large-scale robberies, suspicion quickly falls on a member of the British aristocracy. It seems that his wild-life park may be a clever disguise for his criminal operation rather than an unusual tourist attraction.

At first, everything seems fairly straightforward, then Biggles and his friends stumble on the French connection and straight into – trouble!

KNIGHT BOOKS

BIGGLES AND THE BLUE MOON

CAPTAIN W. E. JOHNS

Lin Seng has the reputation of being one of the richest men in the world, so Biggles is not the only one aware of the value of his astounding collection of pearls. To protect them from thieves, Lin Seng has decided to place them safely in the Bank of England, using Biggles as a courier.

But when Biggles and Algy arrive to collect the pearls, they discover Lin Seng's house and grounds under siege. Others are after the pearls as well, and they won't stop at murder to get them!

KNIGHT BOOKS